THE FIRST TRAIL DRIVE

J. D. WINTER

M. EVANS AND COMPANY, INC.
NEW YORK

M. Evans and Company, Inc.
216 East 49th Street
New York, New York 10017

Library of Congress Cataloging-in-Publication Data

Winter, J. D. (Joe D.)
    The first trail drive / J.D Winter. — 1st ed.
      p.   cm. — (An Evans novel of the West)
    ISBN 0-87131-764-8 (c1) : $18.95
    1. Southern States — History — Revolution, 1775–1783 — Fiction.
2. Cattle drives — Southern States — History — 18th century — Fiction.
3. Cattle drives — Texas — History — 18th century — Fiction.
I. Title. II. Series.
PS3573.I5368F57   1994
813'.54—dc20   94-29363
                                                 CIP

Book design by Charles A. de Kay
Typeset by Classic Type, Inc., New York City
Manufactured in the United States of America

First Edition

9 8 7 6 5 4 3 2 1

This book is dedicated to
my daughter, Jodie, who got me started,
and my wife, Rozan, who allowed me to finish.

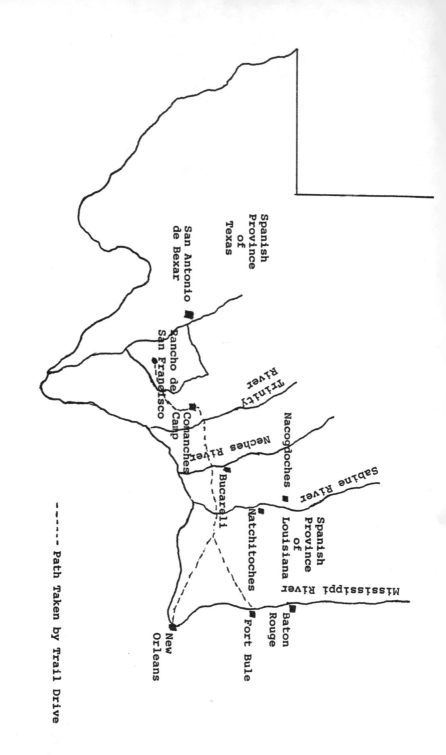

Path Taken by Trail Drive

Spanish Province of Texas

San Antonio de Bexar

Rancho de San Francisco

Comanches Camp

Trinity River

Neches River

Nacogdoches

Sabine River

Bucareli

Natchitoches

Spanish Province Of Louisiana

Mississippi River

Fort Bule

Baton Rouge

New Orleans

Chapter One

THE INDIANS JUMPED BEN CROSS at mid-morning; they came out of the ground like ghosts, dusty from the sand where they had waited for him to enter their circle of death. An arrow creased the flank of Ben's horse, causing the horse to spring forward so the other shots missed their mark.

At least six Indians were around him and he didn't waste time on heroics. He dropped the reins to his pack animals and dug his spurs into the big roan.

Another arrow whistled past his ear and a huge brave grabbed at his horse. Ben slashed down with the barrel of his gun and saw blood spurt from the buck's smashed nose as the man fell away. Then he was clear, running his horse all out.

He made it to the rocks, but Indians were waiting for him. There were only two, and both missed their first shots. They didn't get a second. The deafening blast from Ben's pistol filled the small hollow; blood and bone fragments splattered from the chest of the first brave as the force of the ball threw him backward. The second warrior leaped from the rocks, but Ben dodged to the left and swung the still-hot gun barrel at the head of the Comanche. He heard the sickening thud of his weapon as it landed and the Indian went down.

A spear clipped a rock close to Ben. He grabbed his rifle and spare brace of pistols from his saddle holster, then dismounted and led his roan to better cover.

Ben wiped the blood from the pistol barrel, then re-charged and primed the gun emptied into the brave's chest. He lay his weapons on the rocks in front of him and opened the flashpan of each one to make sure powder was in the touchhole. Satisfied there would be no misfires, he settled back in the shade and inspected the spot where the two braves had hidden. It was a good one—there was no approach from the rear or from above, it had shelter and shade, and a good field of fire in three directions. His guns would keep the Indians out of bow range, so it all depended on how bad they wanted him. He could drop four or five if they came at him in an all-out rush, but eventually they would overpower him. Ben wiped his brow. It was hot and going to get hotter. He had water and patience, so he settled down to wait. The Indians knew where he was. The next move was up to them.

Ben's chances weren't good. Horses like his were rare in this part of the country, and the bucks would take the big roan if they could. They already had his pack animals and might be satisfied with them rather than risk the loss of more braves. Hard to say with Comanches; it could go either way. The Indians knew how to wait, too.

The only thing that moved in the rocks was a lizard that slowly flicked its tongue in and out. The sky was clear but the heat waves that shimmered over the sand blurred Ben's vision.

Time dragged slowly and even though his eyes and ears remained alert, Ben's mind started to drift to the past.

Ben Cross was a wanderer and dreamer, always wanting to see what was on the other side. Only twelve when his parents were killed in the French and Indian War, he'd left his home in the Mohawk valley to follow his Uncle Ezra to the far mountains.

His uncle was a huge bear of a man, with a beard that flowed down his chest and hair that hung below his shoulders. Always dressed from head to foot in animal skins, he was every bit the mountain man. The family had considered Ezra a disgrace because he preferred to wander through the wilderness instead of putting down roots, but he was Ben's favorite. Ben's fondest childhood memories were those occasions when his uncle would return and entertain him with glowing tales about the wild country to the west and the people who lived there.

Ben had used the next sixteen years as a time to learn as well as to grow. His parents taught him to read and write at an early age, but the education he received on the trail with his uncle was of more immediate value on the frontier. He learned to set traps and studied until he could read sign in the woods like words on a page. He honed his senses to the point that he could distinguish between the smell of various animals, as well as those of white men and Indians. Uncle Ezra showed him how to skin the game they caught and cure the hides so they brought top dollar.

They lived off the land and rarely came in contact with other people, except on those occasions when they entered a settlement to trade for goods or sell their furs.

Ben looked forward to the annual gathering of the mountain men at a rendezvous in the Appalachians. They came together to trade, get drunk and swap stories, but mostly to test their skills against one another. They had trials in hand-to-hand combat and in speed and agility. His most favored competition was with rifle and pistol. With those weapons, Ben had no peer.

His father had been a gunsmith by trade and had worked extensively with British army Captain Patrick Ferguson to develop a more efficient rifle. The weapon was finally perfected when Ben was eighteen; Captain Ferguson had found Ben and presented him with one.

The Ferguson rifle was breech-loaded, unlike muzzle-loading weapons used by the other mountain men. One clockwise rotation of the trigger guard dropped the threaded plug in the breech of the barrel. By tilting the weapon downward, the ball dropped into the breech cavity where it came to rest against the lands in the barrel rifling. The rest of the cavity was then filled with powder and the plug closed by a counterclockwise turn of the trigger guard. When the flashpan was primed with fine powder the rifle was ready to fire.

Muzzle-loaded weapons needed a ball smaller than the bore so it could be rammed home, but Ben's rifle used a ball slightly larger than the bore that created a seal when it entered the barrel. The trapped gas from the powder explosion behind the projectile allowed the ball to be ejected with greater velocity, while the tight fit eliminated wobble in the barrel and caused a stronger, truer shot.

His short guns were also breech-loaded. Ben's father patterned them after the screw-barrel pistol brought over from England. He replaced the need to unscrew the barrel between shots with a loading mechanism similar to that used in the Ferguson rifle, allowing the guns to be fired more rapidly and with greater accuracy.

His father died before he could put the pistol in production, so Ben possessed the only models.

Ben's weapons were the last legacy from his father and had not only allowed him to win contests at the rendezvous, but on more than one occasion had been the edge that helped he and Uncle Ezra keep their scalps.

A smile touched his lips as he thought about those wonderful years with Uncle Ezra leading them ever westward, as they trapped and traded with the Indians in the vast untamed wilderness that stretched to the mighty Mississippi River, and beyond.

They found the Spanish provinces of Louisiana and Texas didn't welcome outsiders. The leaders there were suspicious of strangers and feared they might lose their land, but the territory was thinly populated and people easy to avoid.

Ben remembered, as if it were yesterday, the series of events that that brought him to this wild country.

It was in late 1774 as they cleaned traps and watched the early morning fog burn off the river when Uncle Ezra had turned to him and said, "Boy, I figure we been in the wild long enough. Time we took in some civilization. 'Sides, it'll be Christmas 'fore long."

Ben had been thinking along the same lines, since it was over a year since they'd had any news from home. "Sounds good to me. Where to, Fort Pitt?"

"Been to Pitt," came the answer. "Mayhap we oughta go down river 'n see this New Orleans town. Heared it's some kind a place."

"What about the Spanish? They don't cotton t' outsiders."

Ezra loosed a stream of tobacco juice at the fire and said, "Met me a trapper, few months back. Claimed folks down there was hurting for trade goods and paid top dollar for furs. Said Oliver Pollock was in New Orleans—you 'member him. Friend t' me 'n your paw, and one o' the colonies' top leaders."

"New Orleans it is, but I still think it's some risky," Ben had grumbled.

He chuckled to himself as he remembered the furor created when they approached the Spanish outpost out of the mist. What a sight they made, dressed in smelly buckskins grown black with age and grease, hair and beards that blew in the breeze, long rifles draped across their saddles and pack mules strung out behind, they looked as wild as the land they rode out of.

The Spanish sentry stepped out and commanded, "*Alto!*"

They moved slowly forward until the soldier's back was against the guard house, his rifle at the ready, still shouting for them to stop. Uncle Ezra eased one leg over his saddle horn and inquired, "*Buenas días. Habla usted inglés?* Do you speak English?"

"*No comprendo,*" the guard replied sullenly.

Ben waited as his uncle continued, "*Hay alguein aquí qué hable ingles?* Does anyone here speak English?"

The sentry lowered his rifle and answered with pride, "*Si. Mi capitán.*"

"*Lleveme el capitán por favor. Tengo mucha prisa,*" Uncle Ezra commanded. "Take me to your captain, now."

They dismounted and followed the guard to an office in the compound. A young Spanish officer rose from behind the desk and inquired angrily of the soldier, "*Qué es esto?* What is this?"

Uncle Ezra broke in before the sentry could answer. "Excuse me, Captain. Your man here says you speak English."

"He speaks the truth," the officer said, as he eyed them with suspicion. "You are English. What is your business in New Spain?"

"Wal, fact is, me 'n my nephew here are trappers come t' visit an old friend, name of Oliver Pollock," Ezra said. "'Preciate it if you'd fetch him down here t' speak for us. Tell 'em it's Ezra Allen, he'll come."

The officer looked confused, not sure what to do. He finally said, "I will do as you ask, but until you are verified you must surrender your weapons to me."

Ben tensed and turned to face Uncle Ezra, who calmly said, "Fair 'nough, Captain. Like t' get our animals a little water while we wait."

Oliver Pollock arrived as they finished tending to the horses. He was a smallish man, neatly dressed, his stovepipe beaver hat resting on a head of snow white hair. He carried himself in a way that commanded respect much greater than his stature. He set aside his silver-topped cane, then removed a paper from his pocket and presented it to the Commander. "This is an order from Governor Unzaga to release these men in my custody." Then Oliver turned to us and said, "Ezra, it's good to see you. What brings you to New Orleans? Never mind. That can wait."

The Spanish captain read the mandate, then smiled in relief and immediately returned the confiscated weapons and goods.

The ride to Oliver Pollock's residence took only a few minutes and his home, a massive stone structure with an adobe brick wall that completely enclosed the courtyard, was impressive. They turned their animals over to the stable boy, then Ben and Ezra were ushered inside to clean up.

The spicy aroma of home cooking drew the mountain men to the dining room later that evening. The change in them was startling. Gone were the filthy wild creatures of the afternoon. Instead, Ezra's mane and beard were neatly trimmed. Ben's hair was shortened and his face hair gone. Both men were scrubbed clean and wore new tan buckskins. The scent of lilac water that emited from them was not their usual odor.

Oliver smiled at the transformation of his guests, then motioned them to chairs and poured each a glass of *Aquardiente*. He settled back and asked, "How long has it been, Ezra?"

"Near bout sixteen year, I figger," then Ezra motioned across the table and said, "This here's my nephew, Ben Cross. Cora and Zebulon's boy."

Oliver turned to Ben and said, "I was grieved to hear about your parents. The last time we met, you were little more than a boy, but you have grown into a fine looking man. I'm sure they would be proud. What brings you to New Orleans?"

"Thank you for that, sir," Ben said. "I want t' also thank you for your help with the Spanish. We came here t' sell our furs, then relax for a while."

"Your animal skins are no problem. I'll buy them all and pay top dollar. But you may not want to tarry for long."

"What do you mean?" Ezra said, as he sat forward in his seat. "The Spanish don't want us? You seem to be welcome."

"No, no, it's not that," Oliver said. "The governor of New Orleans welcomes traders, and your goods are sorely needed. The problem is at home. I am an emissary to the Spanish from our leaders in Virginia. The pot is boiling over in the colonies. It is obvious the British are not going to meet our demands for self determination. War is imminent, and will happen within six months."

Ben settled back in his chair to absorb the sobering news, then looked across the table and said, "Uncle Ezra, looks like we'll have t' put off our relaxin' for a while. We better get back home 'n teach those Redcoats a lesson."

"'Spect your right," Ezra said, then he turned to Oliver and asked, "Can you get us passage t' Boston? That's fastest."

Oliver replied, "I'll see to it in the morning."

They arrived in early April of 1775. Just in time to join the minutemen at Lexington.

MOVEMENT IN THE rocks below caught Ben's attention. One of the braves had shown himself, just out of musket range, trying to draw Ben's fire. He figured the Indians were familiar with the range of the single-shot muskets carried by most white men on the frontier, and must believe he carried a similar weapon that had only the one shot. Once that was gone, they thought they would be able to move in close and finish him off with arrows before he could reload. The painted warriors had not yet encountered the long reach of his Ferguson rifle, or the double brace of smooth bore pistols he always carried.

Ben smiled grimly to himself. If the Indians kept coming, he'd give them a little surprise.

A brave moved into range and Ben settled the butt of the rifle snugly against his shoulder. He adjusted his aim, slowly expelled his breath and kept his mouth slightly open to help his ears handle the explosion, then gently squeezed the trigger. The hammer dropped and ignited the flash pan, then seconds later, the big gun thundered. Ben recovered from the recoil and stared through the cloud of smoke to see his shot fly true. The lead ball struck and the warrior stopped like he'd run into a tree limb.

Before the Indian's body hit the ground, the rest of the braves, at least ten of them, boiled over the rocks and raced toward Ben's position. Ben abandoned the rifle and scooped up two short guns. He fired too fast with his left-hand pistol and hit a brave in the stomach. The Indian stopped, tried with both hands to ease the pain in his middle, then sank to his knees. Ben aimed more carefully with his right gun and dropped a charging buck with a bullet to the chest.

The hollow around Ben was a cloud of gunsmoke, the smell of sulfur and burning charcoal heavy on the air. He brought up his remaining two weapons, but found no target. The Indians had vanished into the rocks.

Ben quickly reloaded and recharged his weapons, then waited for the attack to resume. He sighted movement near the bodies of the fallen braves and moved his rifle in that direction, then decided to allow the bucks to retrieve their dead.

The Indians came into view out of rifle range, and after a quick conference with a late-arriving brave, they gathered up the pack animals and moved off to the west.

Ben suspected a trick and stayed put, then saw the reason for the Indians hasty withdrawal. A body of horsemen topped a far ridge, dusting it in his direction.

The heat waves that rose from the arid sand blurred the shimmering figures of the riders, but Ben finally recognized the big bay in the lead as Uncle Ezra's mount and relaxed. He was safe now, or would be when they reached him. Ben took a drink from the canteen, then settled down to wait.

Chapter Two

THE RIDERS KICKED UP A cloud of dust when they entered the draw, then Ezra dismounted and said gruffly, "You was cornered like a 'coon up a tree, boy. How come you let yourself get trapped?"

Ben grinned as he took his uncle's extended hand and replied, "Plum carelessness on my part, I guess. You made a mighty pretty sight comin' over that hill. How'd you know I was in trouble?"

Ezra sent a stream of tobacco juice at a nearby lizard and said, "Didn't. Got a message from Oliver that he needs us in New Orleans and I come out t' get ya."

Ben watched the reptile scurry out of sight, then asked, "Any idea what he wants?"

"'Spect he'll tell us when we get there," Ezra said with a shrug of his shoulders. "Boat's ready."

They went down river and found Oliver Pollock waiting for them when they docked in New Orleans.

He greeted them as they left the boat. "I'm glad you are both safe. We've had no word from upriver for days and I feared we lost you to the storm."

Ben looked around and found the dock area a shambles. Workmen were clearing smashed timbers and uprooted pilings. Some buildings were down, others badly damaged.

Ben smiled as he gripped the older man's hand and said, "We got lots o' high wind with the rain that hit us, 'n some

16

spots upriver were pretty torn up, but nothin' like this. What happened here?"

"A *huracán*, and I'm afraid this isn't the worst of it," Oliver replied sadly. "The reports coming in from south and west of here are of total devastation, but the full extent of damage, or loss of life, won't be known for days."

Ben waited as Oliver continued, "The supplies I had for shipment to George Rogers Clark were destroyed, so those already delivered will have to last him the summer."

We won't be goin' upriver for a spell then," Ben inquired.

Oliver smiled and said, "You and Ezra get some rest. I will have need of you soon. Now, can I buy you all a drink?"

They went to the *cantina* in the hotel. Ben looked around the smoky room, crowded with refugees from the storm, and noticed five Spanish soldiers at a corner table. The men were gathered around a sergeant with a knife scar that dissected one eyebrow and trailed down his face, and from the number of empty glasses in front of them, the men were well on their way to being drunk. The uniforms the men wore were not those of the local garrison.

Oliver left after just one drink, but Ben and Ezra remained in the saloon.

"That there's smooth," Ezra said, as he wiped his mouth after his glass was drained. "I'll get us 'nother."

Ezra had to pass the table where the soldiers sat on the way back and one of the men picked that moment to lunge back in his chair. Ezra's arm was hit and the contents of the glasses he carried sprayed down the front of the big sergeant.

The scar-faced man came out of his chair with a roar and clubbed Ezra behind the ear with a huge ham of a hand, sending him crashing to the floor. The sergeant drew back his boot to kick the dazed Ezra in the face, but Ben stepped between them and said, "Stop."

The big man didn't reply, instead he launched a round-house swing at Ben's head. Ben ducked the blow and buried his right fist deep in the sergeant's belly. The other soldiers boiled from their chairs to come to the aid of their companion, and the sheer weight of numbers forced Ben against the bar near the dining room. He knocked one man down, but two more took his place.

Ben's attention was momentarily distracted by a face that looked over the half-door to the dining area as he struggled to throw a man from his back. It was the face of a girl. The most beautiful woman in the world, Ben thought to himself, seconds before a bottle crashed against the side of his head and he went down.

The throbbing of his brain startled Ben back to awareness. He was on a bed with clean sheets, but he wasn't sure where.

He sat and looked around to find Uncle Ezra on a bed beside him and asked, "You all right? How'd we get here? What happened downstairs?"

Ezra held up his hand. "Hold on, hoss. Everthin's fine. Officer broke up the fight and marched them soldier boys off, then helped us up here t' our rooms. 'Pologizing all over hisself, he was. Reckon I'm okay, 'cept for a bump on the head."

Ben grabbed his uncle by the shoulders, then sat back down, his head still in a buzz, and asked, "Did you see her?"

"See who?" Ezra asked. "That blow shake somethin' loose in your head? What're you talkin' about?"

"The girl watchin' the fight from the dinin' room. She's the prettiest thing I ever saw. I've got to find her."

Ezra gave his nephew a strange look, then snorted, "We ain't gonna find anythin' right now but a thick steak t' wrap our bellies 'round. Girl can wait."

The next few days were a frenzy of activity for Ben. He searched everywhere but still hadn't located the mysterious woman from the dining room by the time Oliver Pollock summoned he and Ezra to a meeting with the governor.

The Palace was located on high ground, and had escaped the worst of the storm. Oliver and Governor Galvez were examining maps spread over a massive oak table when

Ben and his uncle were ushered into the richly appointed meeting room.

The governor turned and greeted them warmly, "Come in, gentlemen. I understand your trip up the Missisippi was a huge success."

Ben considered the man in front of him with open admiration. Bernardo de Galvez was a robust, vital man. Although rotund in stature, his dark eyes held the gleam of a warrior. Governor of New Orleans since January of 1777, Galvez had aided the American cause by sending large amounts of arms, ammunition, and supplies, not only to the northern posts of George Rogers Clark, but to the Pennsylvania and Virginia fronts of George Washington's Continental Army. Furthermore, the governor had done all he could to weaken the British along the Gulf coast and up the Mississippi.

"Yes sir, we got the goods through," Ben said. "They were greatly appreciated and much needed. Colonel Clark's campaign goes well, but he'll need blankets and warm clothes for his men 'fore winter."

"Excellent, excellent." The governor motioned them to be seated, then said, "Mr. Clark will have what he needs. Now that you have shown the way, others will manage that. We have a greater problem here that requires your help."

Ezra sipped his coffee and asked, "What might that be?"

"As you know, my government and I, myself, have great sympathy for the colonies struggle against the English. I have it on good authority that Spain will declare war against Great Britain within the year. When my country has made its intentions public, I plan to move against the British strongholds on the Mississippi at Manchac, Baton Rouge, and Natchez."

Galvez spread the map so the men at the table could see, then continued, "I also expect a mandate from my king to expel the English, not only from the banks of the Mississippi, but from the Gulf of Mexico as well. Patrick Henry, governor of Virginia, has assured me the colonies will support Spain's retaking of East and West Florida, areas we lost to the British in 1763. To do that I must launch an extensive campaign against the forts at Mobile and Pensacola."

"Excuse me, Governor," Ben interrupted. "These plans to roust the British are all well and good—and fine plans they are—but what have they to do with us?"

Galvez paused to light a cigar, then turned back to Ben and said, "Mr. Pollock informs me that you and your uncle are familiar with the territories to the west of here. Does that include the Spanish province of Texas?"

Ben thought carefully before he answered. The king of Spain had declared the borders of Texas closed to all non-Spanish people. He didn't want to admit he broke any laws. "Could be we've been over some of it. Hard t' tell where the boundaries are."

The governor studied the man in front of him, then smiled and said, "We'll come back to that later. First let me explain my problem. To mount the kind of campaign I envision, I must have an unending supply of rations for my men. I had such a source, thousands of cattle that grazed in pastures less than a days ride from here, but the *huracán* destroyed the herd and only a few head remain. For me to put my plans into operation, this source of food must be replenished."

Galvez paused as he noticed the puzzled look on the two men's faces as they politely listened, then said, "There are tens of thousands of cattle running wild in the area around San Antonio de Bexar in the province of Texas. I want you to lead a secret expedition and bring back enough animals to restock my herd here. I have written to the governor of Texas and my king for permission to import the cattle, but approval will be slow to come and I cannot afford to wait."

Uncle Ezra leaned forward and asked, "By secret, you sayin' your own people won't be in on it?"

"That is the case, I'm afraid. Trade is prohibited between the provinces of Texas and Louisana at the present time. This will be corrected, but with the first herd you will be outside my protection until you are back across the Sabine River."

"I don't see how we'd be much good to you, sir," Ben said. "The closest I been to herdin' cattle was the milk cows we had when I was a kid. I moved them from the pasture to the barn, 'n Uncle Ezra know's less'n me."

The governor smiled and said, "You won't be expected to actually drive the cattle," then paused as a well dressed young man entered the room.

Uncle Ezra stood up and said, "I'll be jiggered. The fella what broke up the fight the other day."

Ben studied the new arrival. He was about Ben's age, with broad shoulders and narrow horseman's hips. A handsome man, he would almost be called pretty if not for the neatly trimmed mustache. The jaunty grin and twinkle in his eye spoke of openness. Something about the man's face was instantly familiar to Ben, yet he was sure he'd never seen him before this moment.

"You have met then," The governor said.

"Not exactly," Ben replied slowly.

"Then, may I present Lieutenant Joseph Felix Menchaca. He is on detached duty to me from the *Presidio San Antonio de Bexar* in the province of Texas. The *Rancho San Francisco* belongs to his family and is large enough for you to gather the required cattle without arousing suspicion. He and his *vaqueros* will help you assemble the herd and drive it back here. Your job will be to find a way for the cattle to leave Texas without being detected and to protect them from attack."

"Sounds right simple, don't it," Ezra said sarcastically.

"I do not try to minimize the undertaking," Galvez implored. "It is of classic proportions. A thing that has never before been attempted. The cattle you must round up are not docile creatures. They have long, looping horns and have survived on their own for years in a harsh land. Once the herd is formed, you must move it over uncharted territory to avoid any contact until you are out of Texas. The Indians will most assuredly discover your passage through their land, and if the British find out about your mission, they will try to stop you. I'm not making light of the endeavor, but we believe you can get the job done. Our success in opening our offensive against the English depends on it."

Ben turned to Joseph and said, "Guess those soldier boys from the cantina are your men, and they'll be going with us."

"Yes, they are on detached duty also. I must apologize again for that incident. They are good men, but were drunk and mourning the death of the sergeant's mother in the *huracán*."

"The one with the knife scar?" Ben asked.

"That is the man, but the scar is not from a knife. It was acquired in a confrontation with a longhorn steer."

Chapter Three

THE FIRST RAYS OF THE new day's sun filtered through the cracks in the barn when Ben and Ezra entered the stable the next morning. They found Joseph Menchaca and his men had already saddled the horses and were loading the pack mules. The mounts supplied by the governor were fine animals. Uncle Ezra drew a fast-looking bay, and Ben a roan with a blaze face that stood all of sixteen hands.

Joseph turned from his chores and said, "Good morning, *señors*. We are prepared to take the trail when you are."

"Soon as we're loaded," Ben said. He moved to the roan and slung the holsters with his spare brace of pistols in front of the saddle, then attached the buckskin sheath that contained his rifle under the right stirrup, butt to the rear, and tied his bedroll to the horse. Uncle Ezra was already mounted, so Ben lifted himself into the saddle and said, "Let's ride."

They stayed west of the road to Natchitoches to avoid detection by any British patrols that might be out. The devastation caused by the flood waters of the *huracán* extended more than twenty miles from the coast and although Ben and Ezra ranged far out to the front and side of their route, they saw no one, and by the time they found a suitable place to camp for the night it was full dark.

Ben squatted to fill his cup from a coffeepot suspended on an iron rod over the fire, then turned to Joseph and said,

"Your men seem a mite skittish. Have anythin' to do with that little set-to in the cantina?"

Joseph shrugged his shoulders and said slowly, "It is true, I think. The men feel badly about what happened. Sergeant Gomez has much sorrow about trying to use his boots on the old one, your uncle."

"Don't worry about the old one. He can take care of himself. But, We got us a job to do 'n if we're gonna get the governor his cattle, we have t' work togather. This matter has to be settled. Your men understand English?"

At Joseph's nod, Ben said, "Call 'em up here."

The soldiers shuffled forward, eyes downcast against the glare of the fire.

Ben faced them and said, "Look at me, all of you. There is a thing that must be put to rest. The fight in the cantina was a quarrel among men. Somethin' to be put behind us and forgotten. We hold no bad feelin's. 'Nother time it might turn out different."

Tension drained from the men's shoulders and several of them smiled, but not Sergeant Gomez, who started to walk away.

Ben caught up with him and turned the man around, then said, "Can't we, as men, put this in the past?"

The sergeant's face screwed up in anguish as he said, "It is not you, *señor*. I have much shame for what I do. To stomp an old man is not a thing I can forgive myself for."

Ben studied Gomez for a moment, then said, "You feel bad 'cause you think Uncle Ezra is no match for you, that right?"

Gomez shrugged his shoulders, then pointed at Ezra and said, "It is true, as one can plainly see."

"Uncle Ezra was to best you in somethin', say Indian 'rasselin'. That make you feel better 'bout the fight?"

Gomez drew himself up to his full height and said, "That is an impossiblity. I do not know what is Indian wrestling, but I do not wish to cause your uncle more pain."

"Don't you worry none 'bout that, hoss," Ezra chuckled. "This here'll be an even contest."

Ben spread a blanket on the moist ground and explained the game to Sergeant Gomez. "You 'n Uncle Ezra lay down with your heads at opposite ends o' the blanket. The right side o' your bodies'll touch at the waist. When I count one, you both raise your right leg straight up in the air, then lower it down. At the count of two, you do the same. On three, you try to hook the other's leg 'n throw him, while you keep your shoulders flat on the ground. You *comprendo* the rules?"

"*Si, señor*, I understand, but could not your uncle be hurt when I throw him?"

Ben smiled and said, "Just get ready."

It did look like a mismatch when the two men prepared to do battle. Sergeant Gomez was a head over six feet tall, and weighed close to three hundred pounds, none of it fat. Ezra, not a small man himself, was dwarfed by the sergeant's bulk, but the years in the mountains had pared the man down to little more than sinew and muscle.

On the count of one, each man raised their leg and measured each other. At the count of two, they both tensed and prepared for the final surge. When three sounded, Ezra's body shot into the air until only his shoulders remained against the blanket. He was higher in the air than the sergeant and hooked his knee around the bigger man's ankle, then Ezra twisted to his left as he threw his body back to the ground and flipped Gomez to send him sprawling in the dirt.

The sergeant slowly dusted himself off and shook his head, then a tiny smile tugged at the corner of his mouth and he said to Ezra, "*Muy bueno, señor*, very good, but how is it possible? I am the bigger man, and stronger."

Ezra laughed and clapped Gomez on the shoulder. "Can't argue with that. Matter o' leverage. I'll teach ya. Just hope next time I'm in a saloon fight, you're on my side."

"That is a certainty," the sergeant said, then added, "I would be pleased if you called me Raul."

* * *

THREE NIGHTS LATER, they were camped an hours ride out of
Natchitoches. To avoid suspicion, Joseph had taken his men
in for supplies and fresh mounts while the two Americans
remained out of sight.

Ezra cut a fresh plug of tobacco and slipped it in his
mouth, then said, "Been gettin' a itch 'tween my shoulder
blades last few hours."

Ben threw the dregs of his coffee in the fire and said,
"Felt it too. Somebody's out there, but I never spotted 'em.
Joseph'll be back in the mornin'. I'll look 'round 'fore
dawn 'n see what I can find."

He scouted the area surrounding the clearing before the
first pink fingers of the coming sun streaked into the eastern
sky. Grass mashed flat and broken twigs marked where the
men had been, two of them. Left around midnight, Ben figured, since the place where they'd lain was wet with dew.
Boot prints that led to where the horses were tied meant
they weren't Indians, more than that, he couldn't tell.

Ben started to follow the tracks when the sound of riders
brought his attention back to camp in time to see Joseph and
four of his men enter camp.

Ben stepped from the trees and asked, "Where's Raul?
You run into trouble?"

Joseph pulled up his sweaty horse to dismount, then said,
"There is no problem. We cut fresh sign and Sergeant Gomez
trails a deer to get us some venison. Why do you ask?"

"Someone's tailin' us. I found where two men been
watchin' the camp, could be more. Send one of your men to
get Raul. We best move out 'til we see who's scoutin' us.
Uncle Ezra, track the men that were in the trees. Meet you
at the river. Let's get crackin'."

The column was prepared to leave when the soldier
sent to fetch Sergeant Gomez galloped into the clearing,

dismounted and said, with his eyes wide in shock, "*Mi capitán, mi capitán*, the sergeant, he is gone. We must help him."

Joseph grabbed the man by the shoulders and said, "Slowly, Pepe, slowly. What is it you say? Where is Gomez?"

Pepe took a deep breath and said, "The British have him. I followed the spore of the deer and find where many horses cross. Down this trail were English soldiers. They had the sergeant tied to the back of a horse."

Ben settled into the saddle and asked, "How many of 'em was they, and which way'd they head?"

"I count six, *señor*, and they ride to the east."

Ben reined his horse next to Joseph. "Can't be mor'n an hour ahead. I'll cut their trail. You break camp and follow me. Good chance we'll end up in the same place as those two Uncle Ezra's gonna tail."

Ben dismounted when he reached where the horses crossed the deer trail. Signs of struggle were plain. Leaves scattered at the edge of the path and moss scraped off the base of one of the trees. Ben hoped the lack of blood on the moist earth meant the sergeant was still alive. He mounted and headed east at a trot.

The trail was plain and easy to follow at first, then the tracks entered a creek, but didn't come out on the other side. The silt in the murky water made the bottom impossible to read, so Ben turned upstream, then after half-a-mile of no sign, he returned to the crossing and proceded in the opposite direction.

He found a scrape where the metal shoe of a horse scarred the rocky shelf beside the creek, then discovered the tracks on the far side of the hardpan and figured they were now better than an hour ahead of him.

Ben picked up the pace, but the sun was low in the western sky before his nose detected the faint odor of smoke. He tied his horse to a tree, then dug in his saddlebags for a pair of buckskin moccasins and put them on. His rifle in hand

and spare pistols slung over his shoulder, Ben went forward on foot, then dropped to his stomach and wormed his way to the top of a small ridge when voices sounded from the next draw.

He was careful to avoid detection when he raised his head above the rocks to study the English camp. Seven men and an officer were in the clearing, eating a meal. The aroma of venison stew drifted from the pot on the fire, and a deer carcass hung from a tree. "Probably the one Gomez was after," Ben muttered to himself.

His eyes moved slowly from side to side until he picked up the outline of a sentry in the rocks below him and another on the far side of the draw.

Ben started to pull back to get Joseph and the rest of the men when a sound in the brush caused him to freeze. He drew back in the shadow of the boulder as his eyes searched the area to his rear, then relaxed and lowered his pistol when the grizzled features and coon-skin cap of Uncle Ezra appeared from the brush.

His uncle crawled up beside him and said, "'Spect your scalp-lock'd be restin' on my belt, if I'd been a Comanche."

"All the noise you made, most likely'd cost you your own topknot," Ben said gruffly, then he asked, "Those two you followed join up with this bunch?"

"'Bout a mile back. Seen they had Raul with 'em. Been waitin' for you to catch up."

A scream sounded from the draw and the two mountain men scrambled to the top of the ridge to stare down at the camp.

Sergeant Gomez was tied between two trees, his shirt torn open to the waist. But it wasn't Raul who screamed. A soldier, whose hands gripped his crotch, lay doubled up in pain at the feet of the bound man.

Ben grinned at Uncle Ezra. Soon, however, they had to watch in frustration as the English captain cruelly grabbed Raul by the hair and savagely hit him in the face. The sickening crunch as the nose gave way was as loud as a snapped branch. Next, the officer took a knife from his belt and drew the point across the sergeant's chest. The blade left a trail of blood from shoulder to waist.

"Bastard," Ezra muttered, as he fitted the butt of his rifle to his shoulder.

Ben touched his uncle's arm and said, "Not yet. Joseph and his men'll be close, but there's no time to wait. You take the guard on the other side o' camp while I get the one over here. When you're ready, I'll drop the officer."

"Got the man in the trees spotted," Ezra said. "Take me a spell to work behind him. You hear me hoot like an owl, open the ball," then he pulled back from the ridge.

Ben lay his rifle and pistols behind the boulder, then placed his knife between his teeth and silently inched down the slope toward the English sentry. He wasted precious moments when, halfway to his target, a rabbit flushed from the brush and alerted the guard. He was finally in position a few feet behind the soldier and he paused to check the camp.

There was little movement down there. The soldiers were sprawled on their blankets except for two that stood beside the officer who worked on Sergeant Gomez.

Raul hung limp now, only the rawhide thongs around his wrists prevented him from falling to the ground. Blood stained his pants and dripped down his legs from the tracings of the knife that crisscrossed his chest.

The flickering firelight didn't penetrate the dark night enough for Ben to see to the other side of the clearing, but he figured Uncle Ezra was in place.

He rose up and clasped his left hand over the sentry's mouth, then pulled the head back to slice his blade across the exposed throat. The coppery smell of blood mingled with the gases that were released from the dead man's body.

Ben retrieved his weapons and was settled in place when the familar hoot of an owl sounded from across the way. He cocked his rifle. looked down his sights, then squeezed the trigger. The explosion sent flame and smoke bellowing from the muzzle. The lead ball struck the officer just below the nose and the man's face disappeared in a spray of crimson.

Ben lay his rifle aside and raised his pistols, then a shot sounded from Uncle Ezra on the other side—a soldier opened his mouth to scream, but no sound came out; his hands tried in vain to stop the flow of red from the wound in his throat. The rest of the men in camp scrambled for cover and shot their muskets blindly in the dark.

The boom of guns was deafening and the smoke that filled the clearing made it hard to see. Ben aimed at a man who ran for cover, but fired too quick and missed, then a shot from Uncle Ezra cut the runner down.

The rest of the English broke for their mounts when a volley of shots erupted from west of the camp as Joseph and his men rode into view. Ben lined up on a soldier's back, but had a flash in the pan that caused the gun to misfire. The man made it to his horse.

The stench of death collected in his nostrils when Ben moved across the clearing to where his uncle had cut the rawhide thongs and lowered the limp body of Sergeant Gomez to the ground.

Ezra checked the unconscious man, then looked up and said, "Lost a site o' blood, but pulse's strong. Got me some bear grease for the cuts. That'll fix 'em up."

Joseph walked up to Ben and said, "I apologize for being late, although it doesn't look as if you needed much help."

Ben rose to his feet and said, "Couldn't wait any longer. They was treatin' Gomez bad. Didn't act like they was expectin' trouble. What's the count on the British?"

Joseph answered solemnly, "There are five dead and two wounded. The injured will survive."

Ben walked to the fire and studied the ground, then asked, "All of 'em wearin' boots?"

Joseph looked puzzled and answered, "Yes, of course. Why do you ask?"

Ben pointed to the ground and said, "Moccasin tracks, and they ain't mine or Uncle Ezra's. 'Nother thing, eleven horses came into the draw. Only nine in the remuda when we hit 'em."

"Perhaps some of the soldiers wore moccasins."

Ben motioned toward the ground and said, "An Indian left these. See how the toes of these prints point inward. A white man's toes point out."

"So the British have Indians with them," Joseph said.

"Looks like," Ben said slowly. "In any case, we know some soldiers got away. No way to know where they'll have t' go for help or how long it'll take 'em to get back. Patch up the wounded 'n leave 'em food and water for three days."

He turned to Ezra and said, "Cut some long poles. We'll rig a travois for the sergeant. Feel safer on the other side o' the river."

Ben told one of the men as they were ready to leave, "Bring the rest of that deer. Ours anyway—I feel like some venison tonight."

Chapter Four

THEY MOVED THROUGHOUT THE NIGHT and came out of the Sabine river into the province of Texas in the early morning haze of first light.

Ben took special care to hide their trail. The travois was a problem. It not only slowed them down, but the poles dug in and left ruts when they passed over soft ground. He padded the ends with brush, but, in spots, he still had to clean up after they passed.

They stopped to give the horses a blow and Uncle Ezra came up to Ben and said, "Heard the British recruited some Pawnees for scouts. Them tracks back there might belong t' them."

"Could be you're right. Been thinkin' the same thing. There's no way we can hide our trail from someone who can read sign. I'll backtrack and leave a false trail. Try to make 'em think we didn't cross the river. You camp up ahead 'n rest 'til I catch up."

Ben found no evidence of close pursuit, so he splashed back across the river far upstream and circled back. The sun was low in the sky by the time he topped a rise and saw Uncle Ezra at the edge of a clearing. The camp site was a good one, well back in a grove of trees that overlooked the trail.

Ben dismounted and accepted a cup of coffee, then said, "No sign of 'em. We're clear for now. How is Sergeant Gomez?"

"He's awake, but hurtin'," replied Uncle Ezra. "Won't feel like ridin' for awhile, but his chest'll heal. The British wanted to know why we're goin' to Texas. That's why they cut him. He didn't tell. Any sign o' the scouts?"

Ben squatted down on his haunches and said, "They're back there, all right. Two of 'em. I rode back to the British camp and scouted around. Found where horses were tied off out in the brush. Moccasin tracks all around. Trail led off to the east. No way to know if they circled back, but I figger they'll be along."

"I reckon," Ezra said, as he nodded his head, then spit in the fire and added, "Joseph wants t' see you. Got hisself a problem."

Ben turned to Joseph and asked, "What's wrong?"

"I learned in Natchitoches that my cousin left for the *rancho* with only her driver and one outrider. We could have caught up with them before they reached Indian country. Now I fear for her safety if we wait for Sergeant Gomez to mend, or we are slowed by the travois."

Ben said slowly, "See what you mean. What's she doin' out here without an escort?"

Joseph shrugged his shoulders and said, "My cousin is a very headstrong woman."

Ben pulled up a log and sat down, then said, "Complicates things. No way for us to split up with the British on our tail—too dangerous. Only one thing we can do."

FOG ROLLED IN from the river and it was a dark starless night. Ben could barely make out the dim shapes of Uncle Ezra and the soldiers as they left the clearing. A dummy that consisted of Ben's spare clothes stuffed with sticks and grass rested in the saddle of his horse. Ben's coon-skin cap topped the disguise and should fool anyone who wasn't up close, at least he hoped so.

Ben was nestled down in some rocks above the camp. He had his rifle and one brace of pistols, but the weapon he planned to use was the short hunting bow and quiver of arrows that rested at his side. His face and hands were blackened against glare and he wore moccasins instead of boots.

He smiled grimly as the riders disappeared in the gloom. Uncle Ezra hadn't wanted Ben to stay behind, but finally admitted the plan was a good one. A man alone, if he was lucky and very, very good, would have a chance to ambush the Indian scouts and slow down the British.

Uncle Ezra would leave Sergeant Gomez, along with a man to guard him, and Ben's horse at a secluded cave they'd used before. The place was only a couple of miles down the trail and would allow the others to go ahead and catch up with Joseph's cousin before she reached Comanche country, then Ben could bring the sergeant along in a day or so.

His eyes swept the area below as sunlight started to filter through the trees and thin the fog. His position was good and he'd be able to spot anybody who entered the clearing from either up or down the trail.

BEN SQUINTED HIS eyes and looked up at the sun, now high in the sky. It was almost noon and nothing had moved all morning but the birds and a few rabbits. He slowly wiped the sweat from his eyes, took a deep breath to relax his nerves, then tensed as movement in the brush at the edge of the clearing caught his attention. A fox, followed by its mate, moved into the clearing to scavenge and he relaxed for a moment.

Ben's brow wrinkled in worry. If the scouts didn't show up pretty soon, maybe they weren't coming. He decided to give it two more hours.

He stretched carefully, one limb at a time, to relieve the cramps in his muscles caused by inactivity, then froze in place when three robins flushed near the camp. Ben's eyes narrowed as he concentrated on the area beneath the trees and spotted movement. A slight shift of the tall grass against the prevailing breeze, and finally the outline of a man, then another, appeared in the shadows.

Ben's heart picked up a beat as he nocked an arrow and waited for a clear shot as the figures moved into the open less than a hundred yards away.

Ben drew his bow full back, then took a deep breath and loosed the arrow. The feathered shaft buried itself in the chest of the first Indian. The body hit the ground with a thud, and Ben had another arrow ready, but before he could fire, his bow string snapped and the second Indian sprang to his right into the trees with reflexes quicker than Ben thought possible.

Ben dropped quickly to his belly in the rocks and carefully pushed a mesquite branch to one side so he had a clear view of the clearing, saw no movement, heard no sound.

The British would be close, so Ben couldn't risk a gunshot, but the Indian that escaped into the brush had a musket and wouldn't hesitate to fire.

He drew his knife and crawled through the tall grass to the edge of the trees, then stood and peered around a huge oak before he moved silently into the thicket.

Thirty feet into the trees Ben paused when he heard the brush rattle to his left and when he turned in that direction, the near naked brave stood in the shadows with his musket nearly in position to fire.

Ben continued his turn and released his knife in an underhand throw. The blade sliced into the Indian's neck and severed the man's jugular. The brave was dead on his feet.

Ben carried the bodies into the clearing, where he scalped both, then propped them up with their backs against each other in the center of the camp site as a present for the Redcoats.

He returned to the rocks for his weapons, then bellied down behind some mesquite bushes as a large British patrol appeared on the trail.

The Redcoats entered the campsite and dismounted. Ben was too far away to hear what was said, but the two officers were obviously agitated by the grisly discovery of the bodies. They shouted orders, but their men hardly noticed. The soldiers milled around and stared nervously at the edges of the clearing, their muskets pointed at unseen foes.

Ben watched the British place the bodies in a shallow grave, then waited for them to settle in for the night. A canvas tent was erected for the officers, then two sentrys were assigned. He made sure he knew the guards' routine and where they were located, then smiled grimly and moved to a bed of moss where he curled up and went to sleep.

Darkness surrounded Ben when he opened his eyes. He watched the stars high above blink in and out of the low drifting clouds for a moment, then moved into position. The British camp was dark, the fires burned down to coals.

Ben left his guns in the rock and silently worked his way to the trees around the camp. He drew his knife, then eased down to the ground and crawled to within a few feet of the closest guard.

The sentry was half asleep in the shadows. He sat with his back against a tree, musket placed loosely across his knees.

Ben remained motionless for a full ten minutes and detected no movement in the clearing. He made out the dim figure of the guard on the other side of camp, and, satisfied he couldn't be seen from over there, Ben inched up behind the soldier in front of him and clamped his left hand over the sentry's mouth while he sliced the razor-sharp edge of his blade across the man's exposed throat with his right.

The gurgle as blood flowed from the wound was loud to Ben's ears, but no one else noticed.

He propped the dead soldier securely against the tree, then pulled back in the forest and worked his way to the other side of the clearing.

The sentry there was more alert, partly because a pair of playful squirrels in the oak tree above him were shucking acorns and dropping the hulls on the ground near the soldier.

Ben worked his way into position behind the guard and stopped to check the camp, then came up in a crouch and moved forward. A projectile from above hit the Redcoat on his bare head and caused him to stand up and look around.

Only a foot separated the two men when the sentry turned. The aberration that came off the ground at him was the last thing he ever saw. Ben lunged forward and his knife entered the guard under the rib cage, then continued upward until the point burst the heart. The dead soldier's heels twitched weakly against the leaves when his body was lowered against the tree.

Ben moved back to the rocks and retrieved his weapons, careful to cover his tracks as he went, then made himself comfortable in the bushes and settled back to wait.

Shortly before dawn, he was jarred back to full awareness by the sound of shouts from below. He looked at the camp and found it alive with activity with the fires once again ablaze.

Ben eased to his left for a better view and a smile touched his lips as he watched the soldiers load the two bodies, then mount their horses and head back down the trail to Louisiana without even taking time for their morning coffee.

The loss of their scouts and the two dead sentrys had made the British abandon the chase. Ben didn't like to do it this way, but it was important that they get into Texas clean, without any pursuit, so it was necessary.

He followed the Redcoats until they crossed the Sabine River, then turned down the trail and headed west.

The sun was high overhead by the time Ben reached the cave. He approached with caution, then relaxed as he reached a vantage point where he could see Pepe on guard inside the entrance.

He called out, "Pepe, it's me. Don't shoot."

Ben clapped Pepe on the shoulder as he entered the cave and asked, "How's Raul?"

"I am much better, *Patrón*," came the reply from a bed of animal skins in the corner.

Ben squatted down to examine Raul's wounds. The sergeant's nose was still swollen but the cuts on his chest had started to mend.

Ben gave the wounded man a drink of water, then said, "We need to move out soon. Can you sit a horse, or do you want us to rig the travois?"

Raul slowly pulled himself into a setting position and said, "I will ride."

"Good man," Ben said, then he moved to help Pepe saddle the horses.

Chapter Five

THEY MADE GOOD TIME THROUGH the rough terrain that led away from the border and made camp that night on the west bank of the Trinity River.

Ben noticed the character of the land start to change the next morning. They traveled from the swampy area close to the river, through dense forests that teamed with game, and finally into a wide open country of gently rolling hills covered with prairie grass so high it tickled the belly of their horses.

Sergeant Gomez reined in next to Ben and said, "My Texas is beautiful, is it not?"

Ben smiled and looked around him at the grass that swayed in the breeze, then nodded his head. "It is that. What'd you think we can expect from the Indians?"

Raul slowly said, "The land we ride through now is safe. The tribes here are friendly, but that will change when we enter the territory of the Comanches."

"What makes 'em different from other Indians?" Ben asked.

"Oh, *señor*, how can I tell you? The Comanches are devils. They consider everyone their enemy, and do not fight like other men. The braves always paint their face and body before they go into battle, and give screams that chill the blood when they attack. They never fight on foot and, with my own eyes, I have seen them hang over the side of their ponies with just one foot across the horse's back and ride at a full gallop. In this way, the Indian shields his body from the enemy while he fires arrows under the neck of his horse as fast as the eye can see. Another thing, the arrowheads the Comanches use are barbed. They hang in the flesh and must be cut out. They are cruel, ruthless fighters and they torture anyone taken prisoner, then mutilate their victims. They are more feared than any other tribe in Texas."

Ben scratched his chin, then said slowly, "Met me lots of Indians. Found most of 'em to be reasonable people, but sounds like these Comanches are plum ate up with hate."

"It is so," Raul said, then he pulled up his horse, pointed ahead of them and asked, "What is that?"

Ben stared with alarm at a thin column of smoke that spiraled upward to the west, then sunk his heels into his horse's flanks and said, "Too much smoke for a campfire. I'll check it out. You 'n Pepe follow along behind, and ride careful."

Ben heard the boom of an occasional gunshot, then as he got closer, the sound of screaming and yelling like none he'd ever heard. The noise came from over the next hill, so he dismounted and worked his way to the top of the ridge, the last few feet on his stomach.

He parted the waist high grass to peer into the valley below and saw the smoke came from a wagon on fire, one of several being defended against the attack of over twenty painted, screeching savages. The wagons were pulled up in a vee against a bluff in a good defensive position. The Indians rode their horses back and forth at the edge of musket range while they arched arrows toward their enemies.

Ben watched a puff of smoke blossom from a defender, then a brave throw up his hands and slide from the back of his pony.

He squinted his eyes and recognized the forms of Uncle Ezra and Joseph along with several other people crouched behind the wagons. They could hold out unless the Indians came in at an all-out charge. If that happened, the defenders, with their single shot weapons, were too few to survive.

Ben took one last look, then pulled back from the crest to find Sergeant Gomez and Pepe waited below. He hastened to the bottom of the hill and said, "Comanches got Uncle Ezra and the others trapped. We're gonna help 'em."

They rode around the edge of the hill into a gully Ben spotted from above. He figured the dry wash would allow them to get to within a hundred yards of the Comanches without being spotted.

Ben called them to a halt when the floor of the gully started to rise and said, "Check your weapons. We're gonna go out hard and fast, straight at 'em. Don't shoot 'til your sure of your target, then ride through the Indians to the wagons. People there'll give us cover."

Ben placed his rifle in its saddle holster, drew the brace of pistols in front of his knees, then with the reins of his horse clinched between his teeth, he led the charge from the end of the wash.

The Comanches were taken completely by surprise and didn't even spot the three riders until the loud boom of Pepe's musket blasted one of the braves to the ground. The Indians milled in confusion at the unexpected attack. Ben drove his mount at three startled bucks bunched together. Ben shot a brave armed with a musket through the chest with his right hand gun, then a second Comanche's face caved in when Ben's left hand weapon exploded at point-blank range. He replaced his pistols as his horse crashed into the third Indian's pony. The smaller animal went down and the rider fell under slashing hoofs. He saw Sergeant Gomez shoot a brave in the shoulder, but failed to unhorse the buck, then they were clear of the line of Indians and rode for the wagons.

The Comanches regrouped and raced to cut the three white men off, but were driven back by gunfire from the defenders behind the barricade.

They dismounted amid the gun smoke and powder smell that surrounded the wagons to be greeted by the people gathered there.

Ben glanced around, then pulled his rifle from its scabbard and flopped to the ground between his uncle and Joseph.

Ezra looked over at him and said, "Good to see ya, boy. Red devils hit us at mid-mornin', and been pesterin' us all day. We're gettin' short o' water, and I 'spect them Indians was gettin' up the courage for a charge."

Ben reloaded his weapons and watched the main body of Comanches bunch together out on the prairie. They appeared to argue among themselves, then two broke away from the others and charged forward, screaming and brandishing their weapons.

Ben turned to his left and said to Ezra, "Young bucks tryin' to count coup. They keep comin', you take the one on the right."

Ezra sighted in on his target, but suddenly, before they were in range of the defenders muskets, the two Indians veered to the side and rode back to their companions. The two other braves repeated the maneuver while other bucks arched arrows high in the air toward the wagons to try for a lucky hit.

"Stay under cover 'n don't shoot till they get in range," Ben hollered out, as the arrows started to come down around the wagons. "The Indians want us to waste our bullets so they can charge."

The Comanches continued their tactics of harassment for another fifteen minutes and put on a show of riding skill unlike any Ben had ever witnessed. The Indian's taunts failed to draw fire from the wagons, so they pulled back to regroup and plan another strategy.

"'Pears like them bucks got it figgered just how far a musket'll shoot," Ezra said with grin on his face. "But I'll bet me a shiny new dollar they ain't ever run into anything like that Ferguson rifle of yours. Could be, you knock down a couple at long range, the rest'll light a shuck out o' here."

"Worth a try," Ben said, then using his uncle's back as a brace, he drew dead aim on one of the retreating braves.

The Comanche was over a hundred-and-fifty yards away and almost to the main body of warriors when Ben gently squeezed the trigger. His gun thundered and smoke mushroomed from the barrel. For an instant, nothing happened, then the Indian threw his arms wide and tumbled from the back of his pony.

"That was a unbelievable shot, simply magnificent," Joseph exclaimed, as he clapped Ben on the shoulder.

Ezra gave a nod of affirmation and sent a stream of tobacco juice spraying to the ground, while Ben quickly reloaded his weapon.

The Comanches were bunched and milled around in confusion, now over two-hundred yards in the distance. One Indian, bolder than the others, suddenly broke free and advanced to where his companion fell, then stopped his pony and defiantly faced the wagons with his bow held high above his head.

"Looks as if that buck don't believe you can make that shot again, don't it, boy," Ezra said.

Ben didn't answer, instead he stood up and braced the barrel of his rifle on the sideboard of the wagon, pulled back the hammer to full cock and sighted on the distant brave, then fired off the shot.

A cheer went up from the defenders when the lead ball struck the Indian in the chest, and the buck crumpled to the ground.

The Comanches started to pull back, and by the time Ben's gun was recharged, he looked up to find the whole bunch riding away at a gallop.

Joseph climbed to his feet and said, "Indians left so fast, they didn't even take the time to get the bodies of their dead. I'll get some men and put out the fire and see if we can save the wagon."

"They'll be back for 'em, 'less I miss my guess," Ezra said with a drawl. "Most Indians set great store in warriors who fall in battle."

Ezra accepted a canteen, took a drink, then handed it back to Ben as said, "Mighty fine shootin'. Reckon we seen the last of 'em?"

Ben nodded his head, then looked around and said, "They won't be back today. Who are these other folks?"

"These freight wagons joined up with Joseph's cousin before we caught up. Good thing too. Extra guns made the difference 'til you got here."

Joseph walked up as Ben pulled some slack in his saddle cinch so his mount could take a blow and said, "Ben Cross, I would like to present to you, my cousin, *Señorita* Pilar Menchaca and her chaperon, *Doña* Maria."

Ben turned from his horse, his hand automatically going to his coonskin cap. "pleased to meet. . ." he started, then he stood there with his mouth hanging open and stared at the young girl at Joseph's side. His hat fell from slack fingers before he recovered enough to stammer, "I . . . er . . . I'm sorry, mam. I'm glad t' meet you. It was just a shock t' see that it was you. What I mean is, I've seen you before. You were watchin' a fight from the hotel dining room in New Orleans. I tried to find you the next day."

Pilar's eyes sparkled as she looked at Ben, but she replied haughtily, "I can't imagine why you would try to find me, and I was not watching a fight, as you put it, Mr. Cross. I was merely investigating the racket, and I certainly do not approve of brawls or the people who participate in them."

With that, the girl's chaperon took Pilar's arm and firmly led her away.

Ben looked at backs of the retreating figures, then turned to face Joseph. Now he knew why his friend had looked so familiar when he first met him. The resemblance between Joseph and his cousin was uncanny.

Joseph shrugged his shoulders, then smiled and clapped Ben on the back as he said, "I told you my cousin was a woman of strong opinions."

Chapter Six

EZRA AND BEN SAT APART from the others around a small fire when they camped beside a small stream that evening.

Ben poked at the flames while he tried to sort it all out in his mind. He'd thought of little else but Pilar since he first saw her face in New Orleans. Then, when he finally met her, he'd come off like a complete fool, and she wanted nothing to do with him. He thought the least she could've done was give him a chance to explain. "Didn't even thank me for savin' her life," he grumbled under his breath.

Ezra turned to him with a puzzled look and asked, "What'd you say?"

Ben stood up and shook his head to clear it, then said. "Nothin'. Just thinkin' out loud. Guess I'll take a turn 'round camp 'n check on the horses."

Ezra gave a little chuckle and said, "Don't figger you'll be able to walk that gal out o' your mind, 'n ya better not let that there *Doña* Maria catch you sniffin' 'round."

Ben gave his uncle a murderous look and eased into the dark at the edge of the clearing.

The night was clear and bright once his eyes adjusted from the glare of the fire. He moved upstream into a grove of trees, then paused when a splash sounded from the water.

Ben carefully parted the heavy brush with the barrel of his rifle and peered through the opening, then his mouth dropped open in surprise.

Beads of water dripped from the gloriously naked body of Pilar Menchaca who stood in the edge of the stream.

Ben froze in place, but his eyes swept over each feature, every detail of her magnificent figure. She had a very flat stomach. Her body tapered to a tiny waist, then her hips flared out deliciously. Her buttocks were round and perfectly formed. He saw the muscles ripple in her smooth legs when she turned to the side and rewarded him with a clear view of her upturned young breasts, nipples distended from the cold. Moonlight danced over her olive-hued skin and made it appear almost golden in color.

Ben realized he was holding his breath and let it out slowly while he pulled back from the bushes. The chill of the night air on his sweaty brow made his skin feel clammy.

Pilar was dressed and seated on a low rock to put on her boots when Ben next looked through the opening. He started to pull back and sneak away, then stopped as he detected movement in the grass near the girl's left leg. He looked closer at the spot and made out the form of a diamondback rattlesnake, big around as a grown man's arm. The reptile slithered directly for Pilar and she wasn't even aware it was there.

Ben was afraid to shout a warning for fear she might jump the wrong way and a rifle ball might ricochet from the rock and injure Pilar, so he couldn't chance a shot.

He silently stepped from the bushes, then took careful aim and threw his knife. The spinning blade flew true to its mark and buried its length in the head of the snake.

The writhings of the huge reptile in its death throes startled Pilar and she jumped to her feet away from the noise in the grass, then stared first at Ben, then at the snake and back to Ben again.

"It seems I owe you my life once again, Mr. Cross," Pilar said in a low throaty voice, then added, "Tell me, is it a habit of yours to watch from the bushes when women take a bath?"

Ben moved to the snake and used his knife to cut off the reptile's head, then said gruffly, "Wasn't watchin' 'xactly."

Pilar had a twinkle in her eye when she asked, "What exactly were you doing?"

"Look, Miss, I was just out takin' a walk 'n I heard a splash," Ben tried to explain.

"So you were watching when I came out of the water," she stated, with an amused look on her face.

Ben's face was beet red. He shuffled his feet, then admitted, "I was, mam, 'n I 'pologise for lookin', but when I heard the noise, I thought it might be an Indian. Didn't even know you was out here."

Obviously enjoying Ben's discomfort, Pilar asked, "And when you saw I was not an Indian, you looked away?"

This exchange was definitely not going the way Ben would like. Damn that snake anyway, he anguished to himself. If it wasn't for that reptile, he wouldn't be havin' this conversation. He finally stammered, "Soon as I was sure. When I checked back, you was dressed 'n I saw the diamondback."

The flicker of a smile crossed Pilar's face and she asked, "And the reason you . . . ah . . . looked again?"

Ben felt the same way he did when his mother caught him with his hand in the cookie jar, then something struck him as strange and he said, "'Pears to me, mam, you're more interested in makin' me feel like a fool than you are 'shamed about me seein' you like that."

"What do you mean, like that?"

"Well, you know, like . . . er . . . when you come outta the water," Ben struggled to find the words.

"It was not of my choosing that you saw me without clothes, Pilar said defiantly, then she added, "And I am not ashamed of my body. I think it is a very good one. Don't you agree?"

Ben sputtered. He didn't know how to answer that, so he didn't say anything.

Pilar bent down to pick up the carcass of the snake, then said, matter of factly, "As a reward for saving my life, I'll cook this for you tomorrow." With that, she turned and walked back toward camp.

He stood there for a moment, then scratched the back of his head and moved back to the fire.

BEN WAS UP before dawn the next morning, and shaved his face for the first time since leaving New Orleans, then left the camp to scout ahead.

Once away from the river, the trees became scarce and by the time the sun was high in the sky, Ben found himself in a wide open expanse of gently rolling hills covered with waist-high grass as far as he could see in any direction.

A gentle breeze took some of the sting out of the Texas heat as Ben paused beside a small stream to wait for Ezra and the others.

Ezra smiled when he rode up, then dismounted and said, "Gal got a mite upset when you wasn't in camp this mornin' Came around askin' questions 'bout you."

Ben looked at his uncle and asked, "Pilar?"

"That's the one. Seemed mighty curious, too."

Ben looked across at Pilar standing by her buggy, then snorted and said, "Sure don't act that way when I'm around."

Ezra chuckled and said, "That's the way womenfolk are, boy. You'll learn. Spot any trouble?" Then he grinned and added, "That's trouble on the trail I'm talkin' 'bout."

Ben gave his uncle a hard stare before he said, "No Indians. Did spot a big bunch of buffalo west of here, but they were grazin' away from us."

Joseph overheard the conversation and asked, "Is the herd close enough for us get some fresh meat? Buffalo steaks would be a welcome change."

"Reckon so, Ben said, then looked up at the sun and continued, "I should be able to drop a fat cow and catch up with the wagons 'fore dark."

"I will accompany you," Joseph said.

Before Ben could reply, Pilar walked up and said, "And I also."

Ben shook his head from side to side and stated flat out, "No! Wagons can't afford to spare that many guns." Then he turned to Pilar and said, "A buffalo hunt is no place for a woman. I'll go alone."

Pilar stamped her foot and said angrily, "I'll have you know, Ben Cross, I can shoot as well as any man." Then she stormed back across the clearing to her buggy.

Ezra gave a little chuckle, then said, "Regular little spitfire, ain't she," but received no answer.

Ben's eyes were on the sky to check some clouds building in the north when he rode out of camp minutes later. They moved in this direction and he figured they'd bring rain before nightfall.

Two hours later Ben was on a rise that overlooked the edge of the buffalo herd. Thousands of the huge shaggy beasts were spread out in the distance as far as he could see as they grazed on the lush grass and slowly worked their way north.

Ben picked his target, then sighted in on the big cow and gently squeezed the trigger of his rifle. The buffalo went to its knees, then fell to the ground when the ball crashed through the shoulder and into the animal's heart. The rest of the herd took no notice of the loud explosion caused by the shot and continued to feed.

The clouds were black and ominous overhead and the day had become dark, so Ben recharged his weapon, then hurried through the light rain to the carcass and drew his knife. First he made an incision through the thick hide at the base of the skull and cut along the back of the animal to the rump. Then he separated the heavy pelt from the flesh beneath it and made a deep slice along both sides of the backbone to free the sweet meat that rested there.

Ben smiled when he cut out the tongue and held it in his hand. Buffalo tongue was delicious and this one must weigh over five pounds. He placed it, along with the two back straps carved from the cow, on a square piece of hide cut from the animal's skin for transport.

The echo of a gunshot sounded from the west as he tied the bundle to his horse. The rain was heavier now and Ben couldn't see anyone, so he stepped into the saddle and, with his rifle at the ready, slowly moved to investigate the shot.

He topped the rise and looked over, then muttered, "What the hell." Below him was a dead buffalo and Pilar Menchaca worked feverishly on the carcass with a skinning knife.

The only other thing he could see in the gully was Pilar's horse ground-hitched fifty feet in back of her, so Ben nudged his roan in the ribs and started down the hill.

Before Ben reached the bottom, a bolt of lightning shot from the sky, followed in quick succession by others, each one more powerful than the one before, then finally a bolt struck ground to the west that was so bright it lit up the sky.

The frightened buffalo started to move, slowly at first, then in a massive wave that made the ground tremble, and Pilar was directly in their path.

Her horse bolted and ran from the sound as Ben fought to control his mount, then sunk in his spurs and headed for Pilar. He freed his foot from the left stirrup, then once her boot had replaced his, Ben swung Pilar up behind him and, with her arms clasped tightly around his body, galloped down the gully toward a huge outcropping of rocks at its end. They rode onto the jumble of lava as the leading edge of the buffalo herd split and stampeded by on both sides.

Ben helped Pilar to safety on a high, flat ledge, then looked back out over the prairie. What he saw there sent a chill up his spine.

Fire from the lightning still flashed over the herd as far as the eye could see, a thin blue-white flame that danced from animal to animal, seemingly attracted to the horns of the buffalo. The wide-eyed bison didn't seem to be hurt by the flame, just scared out of their wits.

"Looks like the fires of hell. No wonder they stampeded," Ben thought out loud.

He turned to Pilar who stood at his side, trembling. He took her in his arms and held her until the shaking slowed, then asked, "What're you doin' out here, and alone? Why didn't Joseph at least send someone with you?"

She stared up at him, her dark eyes shining, then looked away and replied, "My cousin did not know I came. Sergeant Gomez drove my buggy while I took his horse, then I worked my way to the back of the wagons and when we entered a grove of trees, I dropped off and came back here."

Ben slowly shook his head from side to side, then asked, "But why?"

Sparks flashed from her eyes as Pilar looked him in the eye and said, "You make me angry when you treat me as if I am not your equal. I wanted to prove you wrong."

He pushed her out to arms length, then said, "You don't need to prove nothin' to me. Why, you're the prettiest thing I've ever seen. You're beautiful, 'n I didn't mean to say I was better'n you back there. Just didn't want you in danger."

Her face softened when she gazed back at him and asked, "This means you care for me a little bit, then, does it not?"

The rain had stopped and Ben stared through the dust created by the sea of stampeding buffalo that still surged around the rocks, then turned back and said gruffly, "'Course I care what happens to you. It's my job to get you home safe." Then he walked to his horse and said in a softer tone, "Looks like it'll be awhile 'fore these critters'll let us get out of here. Might as well eat while we wait. Here's some jerky. Hold it in your mouth 'til it gets moist. Make it easier to chew."

Pilar accepted the piece of dried beef and took a small bite, then said, "It is unclear to me, if you care or not."

Ben looked away and muttered, "'Spect we better change the subject 'n get some rest."

He used his blanket to make a pallet for Pilar and placed his saddle at one end for a pillow, then went to a rock near her bed and sat down.

Pilar's eyes twinkled as she moved over in front of Ben and said with a smile, "You are very handsome without your face hair, and I think you do like me some, maybe. Then she bent down, took his face in her hands and kissed him full on the mouth. She ground her lips hard against his, then slightly opened her mouth and touched his tongue with hers.

His head was in a spin and he started to put his arms around Pilar, but she pulled back and walked to her bed, then turned to him and said with a mischievous grin on her face, "Good night, Ben Cross."

Ben stayed frozen in place until Pilar lay down and closed her eyes. Then he moved to the other side of the ledge and, with a grin on his face, muttered to himself, "What'd you know 'bout that."

Chapter Seven

THE MOON WAS HIGH OVERHEAD before the headlong stampede of the buffalo ceased and silence settled over the rocks. Ben looked up at the stars that twinkled down at him from the summer sky, then took a deep breath to draw in the clean, fresh smell of the Texas prairie left on the land by the departed rain.

He woke Pilar when it was light enough to travel, but other than 'Good morning,' she had little to say to him, and not one word about last night. Ben thought she did seem to be in good spirits, smiling and all.

He mounted, then helped Pilar up behind him and headed back to camp. The prairie they rode through was littered with dead and dying buffalo, the weak or lame from the herd trampled by the stronger members. Buzzards already picked at the remains.

"Seems a shame," Ben said as he looked around. "Buffalo keep dying off like this, they'll soon be all gone."

Pilar laughed and said, "You need not be concerned. Their numbers are such that they can not be wiped out. The buffalo will be with us forever."

"Guess you're right," Ben said, then he grinned and added, "Still a waste, though. If Governor Galvez had all this meat back in Louisiana, he wouldn't need any cattle."

The sun was winking over the horizon in the east by the time Ben found the tracks left by the wagons and turned south. He stopped to let his eyes examine the ground after they followed the trail for a few minutes, then looked up to see Uncle Ezra and several riders come over the hill in front of him.

Joseph rode up, a relieved look on his face and said, "Thank God you are safe, Pilar. Are you all right? We've been out of our mind with worry. Where have you been? What are you doing with Ben?"

Pilar started to reply, but was interrupted when Ben said dryly, "Your cousin decided to help me hunt buffalo." He told them about the stampede, then pointed to the ground and added, "We got other problems. Sign here of Indian ponies tailin' the wagons. Only a few, but they could just be scouts. We best get back to camp."

Pilar tightened her grip, then snuggled closer to Ben and said with a smile, "You didn't need to worry about me, Joseph. I've been with Ben . . . all night."

Ben felt the heat start to rise under his collar and didn't wait to see the reaction to her statement, instead he spurred his horse and headed down the trail and the others followed.

They made it to the wagons without incident and found no trouble there, so they broke camp and got ready to move out.

Pilar didn't said anything when Ben helped her down from his horse, instead she squeezed his arm and gave him a big smile.

The smile and squeeze didn't go unnoticed by *Doña* Maria, who stared at the two of them with a frown on her face. She spoke briefly to Joseph, then started speaking Spanish to Pilar in staccato fashion. Ben decided this was a good time to leave and took his place at the head of the train.

They pushed ahead until about noon, then one of the wagons bogged down when they crossed a river and a wheel splintered when they got it unstuck. It was almost dark by the time they finished the repairs, so they made camp.

Ben scouted their back trail and although he didn't spot anyone, he did cut sign of more Indian ponies. When he returned to the wagons, he unsaddled his horse, then went to Joseph and said, "We're still bein' followed. Four or five riders doggin' our trail off to the west."

Ezra walked up and asked, "See who they was?"

Ben shook his head. "Not enough of 'em to attack us, so I figger it's Comanches after our horses. Might try to stampede 'em in the dark 'n pick up the strays."

Joseph spoke up. "What should we do?"

"Hobble the horses 'n tie ropes t' the trees t' rig a corral for the remuda, then build big fires around the herd 'n tend 'em all night," Ben said. "That should keep the Indians away, but post an extra guard. Got us a ways to go 'fore we get to your *rancho*, 'n I don't intend to lose any stock."

Ben spent all his waking hours in the saddle for the next two weeks, away from camp before daylight and seldom back before dark. He ranged out on all sides of their line of march, ever on the alert for sign of trouble. The Indians knew of the wagon's presence in their land, of that he was certain, but sign indicated that no large band stalked the train.

They were two days travel from the *rancho* when Joseph came up to the campfire and pulled Ben aside. Once they were out of earshot of the others, Joseph said, "The freight wagons leave us and turn to the west in the morning. Their destination is the *pueblo* at *San Antonio de Bexar*."

"Been thinkin' 'bout that," Ben said. "If the drivers tell the authorities 'bout what we're doin' here, it'll blow our mission 'fore we get started. Maybe we should keep 'em with us 'til the cattle are gathered 'n on their way."

Joseph said thoughtfully, "I too, have considered this thing, but I believe it would be a mistake to detain the men. I made sure the freighters do not know our reason for being here. They believe I am off duty and on my way to the *rancho* for a visit with my family. Also, the wagons are expected and if they are long overdue, search parties will be sent out and make it more difficult for us to gather the cattle undetected."

"What about me 'n Uncle Ezra bein' in Spanish Texas? Won't your army come t' check things out when they hear two Americans are here with you?"

Joseph smiled and said, "The drivers were told you are old friends of mine and go to my *rancho* to do some hunting, and if a small force does come to investigate, one will be easier to manage than search parties spread out over the countryside. I think it best for us to let the wagons go on their way."

"Sounds like there's no way 'round it," Ben grumbled.

The freighters left the train at first light. There was heavy morning fog all around them, even though they weren't near a body of water and the wagons heading west were out of Ben's sight in a matter of minutes.

He told the others, "Look lively, this fog'll give the Indians cover if they decide t' come after the horses."

The sun broke through the haze before noon and the land they passed into started to flatten out around them. The grass was still lush, but gave way in places to large areas of mesquite trees and thorny brush. Cholla cactus spotted the landscape and in places the chaparral looked impregnable.

The buggy and wagon had a tough time of it when they reached the thick brush. In places where they couldn't go around, the men had to cut a path through with machetes. The Texas sun beat down and made it hot, dusty work. When they camped at dusk that evening, the men were thoroughly worn out. The smell of the last of the buffalo tongue and beans on the fire raised their spirits, but the real cheer in camp was the fact they would reach the *rancho* late the next day.

Ben turned to Joseph and asked, "Land where we're gonna gather the cattle as rugged as what we passed through today?"

Joseph shrugged his shoulders, then smiled and said, "Much of it, I'm afraid. We have vast pastures that are cleared of the chaparral, but the longhorns prefer to stay in the brush."

"Tell me more 'bout these critters we're gonna tame," Ben said with a grin. "The ones I've seen when I been out on scout seemed almighty shy."

"We cannot hope to tame the longhorns," Joseph said. "That is an impossibility. All we can hope to do is calm them down enough to get them to New Orleans. The cattle get their name from the fact that their horns sometimes measure over seven feet from tip to tip, and yet they can run through the heavy brush as fast as a deer. You have seen them. They are huge, rangy animals that have survived on their own in this wild country since before the days of my great-great-grandfather. There are thousands upon thousands of the animals loose in Texas, but they do not run in bunches, instead they prefer to be loners who stay in the brush where their coloring and spotted hide prevents detection. Longhorns fear nothing, even man. The *rancho* has had two *vaqueros* gored to death by them in just this last year, and I personally witnessed a longhorn kill a full-grown black bear that had the misfortune to attack it."

Ben shook his head, then pushed his cap back and said, "'Pears we got a job o' work 'head of us. What about the chaparral. If we got t' go in there after the cattle, that thick brush and mesquite'll cut a horse to ribbons, t' say nothin' of its rider."

Joseph answered, "It will be difficult, but my *vaqueros* have some special items that will make it easier. They will show you how to use them when we arrive at the *rancho*." Then he stood up and excused himself saying, "I think I will turn in now."

Ben went to lay out his bedroll when a noise, one he couldn't identify, alerted him. He slowly straightened up with a cocked pistol in his hand held in close to his body, then the sound came again, "Pssst." The noise came from the edge of trees and his eyes strained to finally pick out the outline of Pilar motioning to him from the shadows.

He moved into the trees beside her and she took his hand in hers, then looked up at him and said, "I only have a moment. *Doña* Maria will look for me soon. Have you told anyone about the night we spent together?"

Ben just stared at her and stammered, "What're you talkin' bout? What night?"

She gave him a coquettish smile, then said, "Certainly not the one by the river. No one knows about that. I speak of when we were with each other, alone, all night. It seems that *Doña* Maria has some very strong opinions about what happened and I thought you might know why."

Ben's head was spinning. Seemed to him, for one reason or another, that happened a lot when he was around Pilar.

He said, "You mean when we got caught in the buffalo stampede. I haven't talked to *Doña* Maria since that night. 'Sides, nothin' happened. You know that, 'n you got to tell her, convince her."

Pilar sighed and said, "I have tried to tell her, but she says I am now compromised and that no man will have me as a wife after I have spent the night with a man, unchaperoned."

"That's crazy, we didn't do nothin'," Ben protested.

"I know that I did not," she said in a querulous voice, "But I was asleep for a time and I'm not well schooled in the ways of the world or what can happen to an innocent girl in the company of an experienced man."

Before Ben could answer, Pilar suddenly smiled, stood on her tip toes to give him a kiss on the cheek and said, "I will do what I can with *Doña* Maria, but she is of the old school and very, very stubborn." Then she was gone.

Ben stood there in the shadows for a moment, with his hand on his cheek, then muttered to himself, "Huh, innocent girl? Experienced man? What was that all about?" He realized his grip on his pistol was so tight that if the gun were not made of metal, it would surely break, so he allowed his muscles to slowly relax, then moved to his blankets. Once in bed, sleep didn't come easy. His mind tried to sort out what was going on with Pilar, but mostly his thoughts were on how beautiful she looked in the moonlight.

The next morning Ben was rewarded with a smile from Pilar at breakfast and a disapproving stare from *Doña* Maria as she shuffled the girl back to her buggy, then the wagons moved out while Ben scouted ahead.

The sun overhead indicated it would soon be noon when Ben stopped on a hill to give his horse a blow. He dismounted and loosened his canteen to let some water trickle down his throat, then gave his roan a drink. His eyes scanned the country ahead, then stopped as a group of riders topped a ridge headed in his direction from two or three miles to the south. He held his position until he could see the horsemen wore high-crowned hats, were fully clothed, and had guns, then he mounted and rode to warn the others.

Ezra halted the wagons when he saw Ben galloping toward them and went out to meet him. He reined in beside his nephew and asked, "What is it, boy?"

Joseph joined them as Ben pulled up his horse and said, "Riders comin' hard from the south. Ten or twelve of 'um."

Joseph looked relieved, then he said, "Surely we can hold off that many Comanches."

"Not Indians," Ben stated, "And this bunch is armed with muskets, not bows 'n arrows. Don't know who they are. We best pull the wagons 'cross the mouth o' that ravine over there until we find out. We got maybe thirty minutes."

They were ready in twenty. Ben and Ezra erased all sign from the trail and cut branches to disguise the outline of the wagons. Ben looked around and decided they were as ready as they could be, even Pilar had a gun. The defenders checked their weapons and settled down to wait.

Tense moments later, they heard the sound of horses in the distance, then they could make out the dim outline of the riders through the brush. Ben watched the men move slowly down the trail, their horses hardly raising any dust. The guns of the riders were at the ready, while their eyes searched the ground for sign.

Ben grimly sighted his rifle in on the last rider in the column. Ezra did the same on the first man in line. Joseph would call out to the horsemen when they came even with the hidden wagons. If the men were enemies, and it came down to a fight, Ben didn't mean for even one of them to escape.

Joseph placed his hand on Ben's arm when the riders drew near, then clapped him on the shoulder as the man in the lead drew even with the wagons and called out, "*Hola!* Carlos, it is you?" Then he turned to Ben and said, "They are not *bandidos*. It is the *vaqueros* from my *rancho*."

The men on the trail milled around in confusion, not sure where the voice came from. One of them called back, "*Si, Patrón*, it is I, Carlos. I do not see you."

Ben moved the branches aside so Joseph and the others could move out onto the trail. The riders all dismounted and removed their wide-brimmed, floppy hats in respect to Joseph.

He acknowledged their gesture, then asked, "How do you come to be here, Carlos?"

"*El segundo* received word that the Comanches were raiding in the north and sent us to find you, *Patrón*. We will escort you back to the *rancho*. A *fiesta* is planned to celebrate your return. I will send a man ahead to tell them we arrive tonight."

Chapter Eight

BEN SURVEYED THE MEN FROM the *rancho*. The *vaqueros* looked strange to him. They were, for the most part, dressed in colorful woven shirts and white cotton pants. Some wore short jacket shirts that came only to their waist, others had on vests, but all the riders sported the big floppy hats they called sombreros and boots with heels high enough to be on ladies shoes. Ben noticed some of the *vaqueros* wore a strange pair of leather breeches over their cotton pants.

When he looked into the men's faces, it was a different story. Ben decided this was a tough and competent group, well suited to survive in this harsh land, each armed with both musket and knife, some with flintlock pistols as well.

Joseph disengaged his conversation with the one called Carlos, then walked up to Ben and said, "The Comanches have been on a rampage, and because of that, the army has stationed soldiers under the command of Ramon Padilla near the *rancho*. I know Ramon. He is a proud and suspicious man. We must not give him any reason to wonder why you and your uncle are here in Texas.

"What'd you have in mind?"

"I plan to inform Ramon that because you saved the life of Pilar, and as a token of my gratitude, I invited you to my *rancho* to relax and hunt mountain lions with me."

Ben thought for a moment, then said, "Might work, 'sept, what was I doin' in Texas to start with and won't the people at your *rancho* know the real reason I'm here?"

Joseph smiled and said, "The Texas sun must have gotten to you, my friend. Surely you remember you saved the life of my cousin while still in Louisiana. As for my people, they will say nothing."

"Might work at that," Ben said with a grin.

Joseph looked down at the ground, then grew somber and said, "There is a thing we must speak of, you and I."

"What is it, Joseph. What's wrong?"

"It concerns you and my cousin, Pilar."

"Me 'n Pilar?" Ben answered in confusion, "What in hell're you talkin' 'bout?"

"It was fortunate that you were there for Pilar that day with the buffalo, but unfortunate you did not get back with her before morning."

"Wait a minute," Ben protested, getting a little mad. "We were in the middle of a stampede with no way to get out. What'd you think happened anyway?"

Joseph looked Ben straight in the eye and said, "You are a man of honor, not the kind of man to take advantage of a woman, so I am sure nothing happened."

Ben looked relieved and asked, "If you know that, what's the problem?"

"You must understand the Spanish culture. It is permitted in our society for a man to have as many women as he desires, even a mistress after he is married, without losing face. But, a Spanish man expects his wife to be chaste when she comes to his bed and faithful to him after the wedding. Any hint of scandal can ruin a girl's reputation and make her deemed unfit for a socially acceptable marriage."

"Sounds to me like your women got the short end of the stick, but, there's no reason for a scandal. Ask Pilar, she'll tell you."

Joseph paused for a moment, then slowly said, "That is

part of the problem, I'm afraid. Pilar has refused to confirm or deny that anything happened. Because of that, *Doña Maria* is certain something did."

Ben slapped his cap against his leg in frustration and asked, "But why . . .why'd Pilar want people to think somethin' that's not true?"

Joseph shrugged his shoulders and said, "I told you my cousin is a strong-willed woman. She believes, as you say, that our women get the short end of the stick and her father has spoiled her terribly. This is not the first time she has caused raised eyebrows, but this time she may have gone too far. I am sure she will eventually admit the truth. I only hope it will not be too late."

"Too late. What do you mean, too late?"

"Paco Ruiz, my *segundo*, has been in love with Pilar since they were both children. Paco is of royal blood. The only reason he works on my *rancho* is to be near my cousin. He is a proud man and I fear he will feel be compelled to defend Pilar's honor."

Having to drive two thousand wild Longhorn cattle a thousand miles over uncharted territory suddenly didn't seem like such a big deal to Ben and he said, "You mean this Ruiz fellow will challenge me . . .over this?"

"I believe this to be so. I will talk to Paco, but it may do no good. He has the loyalty of the *vaqueros*, and any confrontation between the two of you would seriously hinder our efforts to gather the cattle and get them to the Governor."

Ben studied for a split second, then said, "We need Ruiz on our side to get the job done . . .so I just won't fight 'em."

Joseph looked at Ben with troubled eyes and said, "I pray for it to be that simple. In any case, we must leave for the *rancho*."

Ben stared at Joseph's back, then walked over to where his uncle held the horses.

Ezra sent a stream of tobacco squirting toward the ground and said, "You 'n the lieutenant was havin' quite a palaver. Anythin' the matter?"

Ben told his uncle the whole story, and when he was finished, Ezra gave a little chuckle and asked, "How'd you feel 'bout this Pilar gal?"

Ben stared hard at his uncle, then his gaze softened and he said, "Fact is, Uncle Ezra, don't think I know. There's times she makes me so mad I could spit, or pinch her head off, other times I got a strong hankerin' for her. If she was a squaw, I 'spect I'd throw her over my horse and carry her away with me."

Ezra looked at Ben for a long moment, then said, "This 'n ain't no squaw, boy. 'Bout the only thing I never learned you was how to handle women folk. 'Spect that's 'cause I never paid 'em much mind, or had a hankerin' to settle down with a wife. Looks like you picked a good 'n t' complete your education. What're you gonna do?"

"Damned if I know," Ben said slowly. Then he and Ezra mounted and led the way down the trail. Ben glanced toward Pilar's carriage as he took his position, but she was hidden behind the curtains.

He pushed everything out of his mind as he rode. Whatever happened now, would happen. All he could do was wait, then decide how to handle it.

Ben gave his horse its head and let the animal just meander along while he thought about his life. He didn't know exactly what he searched for in all his wandering, but of all the places he'd journeyed, this wild Spanish province of Texas suited him best. It was a fine, rich, wide-open land, with gently rolling hills covered with lush prairie grass, and emerald-green forests that teemed with wild game. This was definitely a country where a man could live and have room to grow, and Ben wasn't getting any younger. Then, he chided himself for even thinking about it. Pilar didn't care anything about him. She was just having fun with him.

Still and all, he thought to himself, it was a beautiful country and the girl wasn't bad either.

Ben was brought back to the present when Uncle Ezra nudged him in the ribs, pointed off the side and said, "Got company."

Two Indians sat on their ponies, and watched them from the ridge, then three more joined them. He looked to the other side of the trail, a band of warriors was there also.

Joseph rode up beside Ben and said, "Indians, on the ridge."

"Seen 'em," Ezra said.

Ben studied the Comanches as they sat there on their ponies, not moving. He turned to Joseph and asked, "We close enough for gunfire to be heard from your ranch?"

"Of a certainty, the *hacienda* is just over the next hill. You can see the smoke from the cook fires."

Ben nodded his head and said, "Tell your men to rest easy, but make sure 'n keep a close watch on the spare horses. Indians won't attack this close t' help. My guess is, it's a bunch of young bucks tryin' to show how brave they are."

Little more than an hour of daylight remained by the time they topped the hill and looked down on the headquarters of the *rancho*.

Uncle Ezra surveyed the scene below, then gave a low whistle, and Ben had to agree with him.

The *hacienda* of the *Rancho de San Francisco* would have been impressive on the outskirts of Mexico City or Madrid, Spain, but out here in the middle of this wilderness, it was truly magnificent. The main house was a massive two-story, white-stone structure with a bright red roof of molded-clay tile. A dozen smaller buildings were scattered around the compound, along with corrals and a hay barn. Ben nodded with approval at the two water wells dug in the clearing, and at the stone wall that stood at least ten feet high and four feet thick that surrounded the entire area.

Joseph led them through the thick wooden gates and they were immediately engulfed in a throng of shouting, happy people. The men were dressed in white pants and shirts, all with hats in their hands. The women wore full skirts with brightly colored shawls draped over their heads.

"Seem right happy t' see us, don't they?" Ezra drawled with a wide grin on his face.

Ben smiled at the remark, but didn't answer as his eyes scanned the crowd. He didn't know Paco Ruiz, or if there'd be trouble, but he stayed loose and ready for action. He noticed Ezra still had his rifle across his saddle.

They made the stable without incident, then turned their mounts over to the horse tender and followed Joseph into the main house.

Ben saw that the inside of the house fulfilled the promise of the outside. The wooden floors were adorned with brightly colored woven rugs. The walls were draped with the same, along with ornate carvings of wood, silver, and gold. Heavy furniture of solid oak was throughout the house, and the eight-foot ceilings kept the inside cool.

Ben and Ezra were shown to adjoining rooms, each with a bathtub full of steaming hot water waiting for them.

Ben had soaked most of the dirt and grime from his weary body when he heard a knock on his door.

He asked, "Who is it?"

Ben pushed himself deeper in the tub and grabbed for a towel as a young Mexican girl walked in and said, "*Con permiso*," then proceeded to place whiskey and a bowl of ice, along with two glasses, on the table. Ben pulled the towel closer to him as another girl entered and laid out a complete suit of clean clothes on the bed, even a pair of new boots on the floor. The girls looked at each other, then, amid much giggling behind their hands, left the room.

Ben listened to be sure they were gone, then jumped out of the tub and locked the door. He mixed a strong drink and started to get ready, and was on his second whiskey when Uncle Ezra came in through the connecting door.

Ben heard him and said, "Don't believe much in privacy down here, do they?"

Ezra chuckled, "As pretty a couple o' interruptions as I ever did see."

"Didn't notice," Ben grumbled as he finished his shave and slicked down his hair.

Ezra mixed himself a drink and said, "You didn't notice? Hells fire, that little gal's got ya hooked worse 'n I thought."

Ben turned around to give an angry retort, but the words stuck to his tongue.

Gone was Ezra's beard and his flowing mane of hair was trimmed short, combed back. Ben couldn't recall Uncle Ezra ever being clean shaven, and the clothes he wore completed the transformation. Ezra was dressed in a fawn colored outfit. The trousers fit tight until they reached below the knee, then flared out to end just above the polished boots. He sported a white shirt with ruffles down the front and black string tie under a jacket that fit tight across the shoulders, then tapered to the waist where it stopped.

With a broad grin on his face, Ben said, "Uncle Ezra, you look down right . . . well, splendid, that's the only word for it, splendid."

"Time I taught you t' mix with genteel folk," Ezra said, "'Sides, you look kinda like a dandy your own self."

Ben gazed in the mirror and saw it was true. The outfit he wore was much the same as Ezra's, only his was in pale blue instead of fawn. He turned to his uncle and said, "Somethin' smells mighty good. Let's go down and eat."

The meal was a real ordeal for Ben. He hardly tasted what food that made it to his mouth, and he didn't have a second helping of anything.

Pilar was dressed in a emerald-green gown with hardly any top to it at all. She looked beautiful, but didn't even acknowledge Ben's presence, at least not openly, although he did see her glance his way several times when she thought no could see. It was *Doña* Maria, though, who made Ben's mouth go dry and ruined his taste for food. Every time he looked up, her piercing black eyes bored a hole through him while her mouth curled down in disapproval.

Ben was the first one out of his chair when supper was finally over and the men retired to the next room for cigars and an after dinner drink.

Several *vaqueros* entered from the veranda as the butler closed the doors to the dining room.

Joseph turned and said, "Ben, Ezra, you know Sergeant Gomez, and Carlos from when he met us on the trail. Now I would like to present my *segundo*, Paco Ruiz."

Ben was impressed when he studied Paco. The man was tall for a Mexican, almost to Ben's height, and heavier by maybe twenty pounds, all of it looked solid. The *segundo* had a broad flat face and a mustache that drooped on both sides of his mouth level with the bottom of his chin.

Ben held out his hand and said, "Pleased to meet ya."

Hatred flashed from the man's eyes and Paco made no effort to shake hands with Ben, or return the greeting.

Joseph's face screwed up in anger and he barked, "Paco, you forget yourself. This man is a guest under my roof."

Ben felt the heat rise under his collar, but he bridled his anger and let his arm drop to his side without speaking.

"*Por favor, Jefe*," Paco said with a sneer, "I do not wish to shake the hand of this *cabrón*, this despoiler of women. I prefer instead to carve his entrails from his body."

Ben started forward, but Joseph stepped between the two men and said, "Enough! Paco, you disgrace my home. Leave me now. We will discuss this tomorrow."

Paco glared at Ben and said, "Another time, *señor*. You will not always have *el patrón* to hide behind. I think you are able to feel like a man only when you face a defenseless woman." Then the *segundo* stormed out the patio doors and into the night.

Silence settled over the room, then as the other men filed out, Ben rubbed his chin and said to Ezra, "Tomorrow oughta be a right interestin' day, what with the fiesta 'n all."

Joseph gave Ben a troubled look, then shrugged his shoulders in despair, then without another word, they made their way upstairs to bed.

Chapter Nine

BEN DIDN'T EAT IN THE main house the next morning. Having to face *Doña* Maria over the breakfast table wasn't his idea of the best way to start the day, so he had the cook wrap some beef and beans in tortillas and went down to the stables. He met several *vaqueros* when he crossed the yard, but the men didn't even acknowledge Ben's presence, just gave him an impassive stare until he passed.

Joseph and Ezra hurried into the stable as Ben finished his meal and started to check the horses.

"Thought we'd find you here," Uncle Ezra said, "We got us a little problem."

"I know," Ben replied, "Paco Ruiz. Hasn't that hot head cooled off yet?"

Joseph shook his and said, "It's more than just that, I'm afraid. Pilar now understands the importance of our mission and promised she will talk to Paco, but it may be too late. The incident between the two of you last night has been blown out of proportion. There is much grumbling among the *vaqueros*, who now question your bravery because you took Paco's insults and did not stand up for yourself. The men say they will not take orders from a coward. I think it is Paco's way to force you to fight. I can order my men to help us, but without their dedication, the drive could be jeopardized."

"Damn," Ben exclaimed. He slammed his fist into his hand, then thought for a moment. What if I fight Paco and whip him?"

"It is not that simple," Joseph said. "I know Paco and the only way you can defeat him is to take his life."

Ezra asked Joseph, "How're your boys gonna take it, if Ben has t' kill Ruiz?"

"No way to know for sure. Carlos would be the one to take over as *segundo*, and he is fiercely loyal to Paco. At best, we would have only half-hearted support from the men."

Ben frowned, then said, "In other words, I have to fight Paco to get the respect of the *vaqueros*, then if I kill him, they won't work for us. On the other hand, if he kills me, you have nobody to guide the herd. Either way, the chances of getting the cattle to New Orleans don't look good. We got to find another way to make things right."

Joseph wrinkled his brow in concentration, then said, "There is one possibility, but it will be extremely dangerous and could also cost you your life." Joseph proceeded to tell them his idea, then left to let Ben mull it over in his mind.

The rest of the day was taken up with fiesta. Preparation of food for the event had been under way all night, and taste-tingling aromas filled the air. Carcasses of deer, goat, and javelina, along with buffalo hump and wild turkey, roasted over open spits, doused with spicy sauces by the cooks.

Lieutenant Padilla, along with a group of his soldiers, arrived for the festivities and Joseph brought him over and said, "Ben, Ezra, this is a very good friend of mine, Ramon Padilla, and Ramon, this is Ben Cross and Ezra Allen, the men I told you about. The ones who saved Pilar from the Indians."

Ben studied the man as he shook hands. Padilla was short and rotund, not over five foot four in height and nearly that in girth. His fancy blue uniform was bordered with gold braid, and he seemed to strut when he walked.

Padilla looked Ben up and down, then said with a sneer, "Of course, the *yanqui* heroes. It is highly unusual for *Norte*

Americanos to venture this deep into Spanish Texas, and extremely unhealthy for those who do so without proper papers."

Joseph interrupted, "As I informed you earlier, Ramon, these men are my guests. I am indebted to them for saving my cousin's life and invited them here to rest and hunt."

Padilla clasped his hands behind his back, then looked up at Joseph out of the corner of his eye. "So you did. So you did. Lion hunting, I believe you said. Well, we shall see. We shall see." Then the lieutenant abruptly turned and walked away.

Ezra hooked his thumb at Padilla's back and asked, "He gonna be trouble?"

"We must be careful," Joseph said, "But it is Ramon's way to be suspicious of strangers. I must go to the reviewing stand now. Will you join me?"

"You go ahead," Ben said. "We'll watch from down here."

Music and laughter filled the courtyard, while the people of the *hacienda*—men, women and children, who were all dressed in their finest and most colorful attire—did their best to eat and drink their fill.

The *señoras* prepared their favorite dishes for all to sample, while the *señoritas* enticed the beau of their choice into a dance.

The children amused themselves in a variety of ways, then topped their day with the breaking of the *piñata*— a game where the children are blindfolded, then given a stick to try and break a clay pot hung over their head filled with sweets.

The *vaqueros* and some of the soldiers competed with each other in all manner of contests, from busting wild broncos to steer wrestling and bull riding. They had tests of strength, but Sergeant Gomez won those hands down, also feats of trick riding and skill with weapons. Ben and Ezra remained on the sidelines during the events, as did Paco Ruiz, who seemed to hold himself above participation in contests with people he considered beneath his station in life.

Pilar was in the spectator stand throughout the day, and visible to Ben, but she was always in the company of *Doña* Maria, so he never had a chance to approach her.

The most interesting contest to Ben was a test of riding and agility called the chicken pluck. In this event, a hen is buried in the ground until only the head remains visible, then a rider, riding at a full gallop, must lean from the saddle and pluck the head from the body of the chicken without losing his balance or falling from his mount. The body of the bird is then added to meat on the grill and cooked in celebration.

The sun was halfway down in the western sky, and the day near to its end, when Joseph walked over to Ben and said, "'The placing of the ring' is the next event. Are you sure you want to do this?"

"Don't see as how I got much choice if we're gonna get the cattle through. Tell me again what I gotta do."

"Come," Joseph said, "It begins and you will be able to see for yourself."

They walked to a large corral that contained more than thirty longhorn steers, big rawboned creatures with long curved horns that extended to a point some three to four feet from each side of their head. The steers were excellent examples of the species and raised a cloud of dust as they nervously pawed the ground and milled back and forth inside the enclosure. One black bull in the far corner stood taller than the others and looked particularly menacing.

Ben's attention was drawn to the far side of the corral when the *vaqueros* let out a cheer, then Paco Ruiz worked through the crowd, mounted on the back of a magnificent white stallion.

The *segundo* cut quite an impressive figure. He was dressed completely in gold, from his boots to his hat, with braid embroidered on his jacket and along his pant legs.

His horse stood a full sixteen hands and was encased from leg to neck in armor made of layered buffalo hide.

Ezra scratched his chin and said, "Looks mighty pretty, don't he? What's his horse made up for?"

"The object of the game is for a person to place a ring, only six inches in diameter, on one horn of the big black bull, and have it remain in place while the man rides away," Joseph explained. "To accomplish this, the rider must weave in and out of the other longhorns until he maneuvers close enough to place the ring. The stallion must be protected, otherwise it will be gored by one of the steers or the big bull and leave the rider at the mercy of the other animals. Paco is the only *vaquero* on the *rancho* who will even attempt to accomplish this. I informed him that you will also try."

"Looks t' be right dangerous, at that," Ezra commented.

They moved close to the poles of the corral as silence settled over the crowd in anticipation of the start of the test of wills between man and beast.

Ben watched Paco enter the ring, and had to admit, the man had plenty of sand in his craw. The *segundo* had the ring in his right hand and loosely held the reins in his left. He gave his horse its head and used his knees to guide the way through the maze of cattle. The stallion pranced slowly forward, and moved in a way that wouldn't frighten the steers and cause them to charge. Several animals, one or two at a time, lowered their heads and pawed the ground, but then backed off and moved out of the way.

Paco worked his way to the far side of the corral. Only a few cattle remained between him and the black bull, then, as he inched forward, the whole bunch bolted and circled to the left around the enclosure, so horse and rider were forced to start the process all over again.

Silence hung heavy around the compound as crowd watched the *segundo* start slowly forward. Every eye was riveted on the arena and the actions of the man on the white stallion.

The cattle were more nervous and skittish now. When Paco moved close to them, the steers tended to jump out of the way rather than just move aside, and raised a cloud of dust that caused tension to rise.

Sweat stained the back and underarms of Paco's jacket as he worked to move ever closer to the black bull. One of the steers lowered its head and charged. That caused the horse to swerve to one side, but the maneuver cleared the way and suddenly the black bull was backed against the fence, hemmed in on both sides by milling cattle.

Paco nudged his stallion forward, and the bull, seeing no way out, plunged forward at the white horse. At the last instant, with riding skill that made Ben whistle in admiration, Paco pulled his mount to one side. The tip of the bull's horn scraped the breast plate of the horse, then when the animal pulled up his head to gore, the *segundo* leaned from the saddle and slipped the ring over a horn. The bull angrily tossed its head and stomped its feet, but the stallion danced to the side and away. The ring went flying, but not before Paco was well back and in the clear.

A round of cheers went up from the crowd, followed by another and still another.

Paco Ruiz acknowledged the praise by removing his sombrero as he circled the enclosure. He paused in front of Ben and said with a sneer, "Your turn," then rode from the corral.

Uncle Ezra spat a stream of tobacco juice at a fence post, then turned to Ben and said, "You still aimin' t' go through with this craziness, I'll saddle your horse."

"No need for that," Ben said. "I'm not gonna take a good horse in there and get 'em maimed."

Ezra stepped back and stared at his nephew, then asked, "That mean you ain't gonna give it a try?"

Ben took the ring from Joseph and picked up a six foot pole with a sharp end, then said, "Naw, just means I ain't gonna have a horse with me." Then he vaulted over the poles of the corral and landed on the dust inside.

All attention shifted back to the arena when the people spotted Ben jump over the bars. A hush fell over the crowd, then a gentle murmuring of conversation that grew into a roar. Ben even heard a few scattered cheers.

He waited for the hubbub to die down, then started to walk slowly forward. Ben used the stick to gently prod the cattle out of his way while he kept the poles of the corral to his right as he worked toward the black bull. One steer made a motion as if to charge, but the sharp end of the stick turned it away.

The cattle milled around in front of Ben as they moved to the left, but the bull was always shielded by other steers. Then Ben saw an opening. He squeezed quickly between two animals and made an attempt to place the ring, but he missed. The bull dodged back and ran with the rest of the cattle to the other side of the corral.

Ben removed his cap and threw it to Ezra, then wiped the sweat and dust from his brow and moved slowly around the enclosure. A brindle steer in front of him stood its ground and stared at Ben out of yellow rimmed eyes, then pawed the ground so hard that clods of dirt flew over the animal's back and into the cattle behind.

The animals scattered and Ben took this opportunity to dodge around the brindle and vault over the rump of another steer to come down beside and a little behind the black bull's head. Ben placed the ring over the animal's left horn and ran to the edge of the corral and scrambled out of the arena.

Ben paused with one leg hooked around the top rung of the enclosure and turned to watch the big black animal. The bull stood still for a moment, then seemed to shudder at the affront, and charged the fence where his tormentor rested. Ben dropped lightly to the ground on the outside, amid the sound of rousing cheers, as the bull crashed full tilt into the corral with such force a man was dislodged from his perch several yards from where contact was made with the fence.

Vaqueros, soldiers, and people of the *hacienda* closed around Ben, all wanting to touch him, to congratulate him.

Sergeant Gomez picked Ben up, gave him a bear hug and said, "*Muy bueno*, my friend. Never have these eyes witnessed anything of such *magnificencia*. This is the only time anyone even attempted 'the placing of the ring' when not on horseback."

Ezra clapped Ben on the shoulder and said, "That's pure, boy, real pure. 'Spect nobody'll doubt your courage now."

Ben glanced over the top of the crowd, and noticed Pilar involved in a deep conversation with Paco Ruiz, then *Doña* Maria hurried the girl away and the man turned and walked in Ben's direction.

The Mexican removed his sombrero, looked Ben in the eye, then bowed slightly and said, "That was a magnificent thing you did in the ring, *Señor* Cross, and I wish to extend to you my apology. It seems I was misinformed about your actions in regard to *Señorita* Menchaca, and there can no longer be any doubt about your courage. I was a fool and it will be understood if you choose to not accept my apology."

Ben smiled, then extended his right hand and said, "Apology accepted. Just a misunderstandin', Paco, I respect your courage and would be proud to call you friend. Has Joseph told you why we're here?"

Paco eagerly pumped Ben's hand, then nodded his head.

Ben said, "I'm gonna need your help to get the job done. Can I count on you?"

You have my word, *Señor* Cross. I will get the cattle to New Orleans for you or die in the attempt."

Ben clapped Paco on the shoulder and said, "That's good 'nough for me. My friends call me Ben, let's go get a drink."

Chapter Ten

JOSEPH AND UNCLE EZRA JOINED them in the *cantina* as Ben ordered a second round.

He signaled for two more drinks, then turned to Joseph and asked, "When do we go after the cattle?"

"Everything is in readiness. We will leave as soon as Ramon and his soldiers depart. Probably in the morning."

Joseph raised his glass to Ben and said, "To you, my friend. You have gained the admiration of everyone. Now I feel very good about our venture."

Paco and Ezra grinned and raised their glasses also.

A smile touched the corners of Ben's mouth as he said, "I was lucky. That was one mean bull." then he changed the subject. "You got a map that shows where the cattle are?"

Joseph said, "Crude ones only, I'm afraid. The fiesta will continue into the night, but as soon as the cloak of darkness gives us cover, we will meet in my office to decide on our plans."

Ben leaned back in his chair to look outside, then said, "Couple more rounds 'n it ought to be dark enough."

Joseph left the cantina before the others to make sure Ramon Padilla was otherwise occupied and did not prowl around the compound.

Ben and Ezra already had Paco's charts spread out on the table by the time Joseph arrived at the office.

He entered the room and said, "We are safe now. Ramon has sent his men to bed with orders for an early departure."

Ben nodded his head, then said, "Show me where the cattle are and how you plan t' gather 'em."

Paco pointed at the map with his finger and said, "We are here. The *Rancho de San Francisco* covers nearly fifty-thousand acres, but only a small portion of it around the *hacienda* is cleared. The rest of the area is much the same as the land you passed through on the way here. Cattle are everywhere, but the greatest number are located here, near the southern border of the *rancho*."

"Why there in particular?" Ezra asked.

Paco shrugged his shoulders and said, "The country there is much like the longhorn themselves; wild and untamed. It is covered with thick brush whose thorns are long enough to rip the clothes from a man's body, and cactus spines that can cripple a horse. Yet even hindered by their long horns, the wild cattle, with their lean bodies, long heavy-boned legs, and thick hooves, move swiftly through the overgrowth at will."

"Sounds like a spot o' work to get 'em out," Ben said thoughtfully. "How we gonna get that little job done?"

Joseph laughed and said, "First, we drive stakes in the ground that are caked with a mixture of salt and tallow. The longhorns come to the smell and my men will round them up."

"Pretty slick," Ben said with a grin. "Reckon it'll work?"

"We have done it before. My *vaqueros* will gather the cattle, but you and Ezra will also be riding through some rough country, so I have some things for you."

He went to the corner and returned with some of the funny looking leather breeches without a seat that Ben had noticed some of the Mexicans wore over their pants.

Ezra gave Ben a puzzled look when Joseph handed each of then a pair and said, "We call these chaps. They will protect your legs and clothes from the thorns in the brush, and I have a jacket for each of you as well."

They examined the garments, then Ezra looked up and said, "They'll do."

Joseph said, "I'm sure you noticed the boots you found in your room have higher heels than you are accustomed to. The deeper heel gives you more stability in the saddle, and will prevent your foot from sliding through the stirrup."

"'Preciate these things. They'll come in right handy," Ben said. Then he asked, "How long'll it take for your men to get the cattle together?"

"'We will have thirty *vaqueros*, each with a working string of five horses," Joseph said. "If they gather between one and two hundred cattle a day, we'll be ready to start for New Orleans in two weeks, three at the outside."

Ben studied for a moment, then pointed to the map and said, "'Reckon I better be findin' us a way to get there then. Tell me about the land 'tween here 'n the Sabine River?"

Paco leaned over the table and said, "The easiest route to the crossing at *Villa de Nacodoches* is along here, but the Comanches moved in there several years ago and have denied us use of that road ever since. The way you came here was to the north of that route and even that direction would not be safe from Indian attack because the cattle will slow us down. In addition, that line of march could cost us an extra two to three weeks of travel time."

Ben asked, "What if we cut straight across here to the east? Seems to me that's the shortest way to the river."

"Unfortunately, little is known about that part of the country," Joseph said. "Even some areas of my land in that direction have not been explored, but as you say, that would be the quickest way. . . if you can find a path that the cattle can follow."

"I'll leave soon as we set up a base camp," Ben said. What about Padilla 'n his men? They likely to scout this far to the southeast?"

Joseph shrugged his shoulders and said, "It is doubtful, but with Ramon, one never knows."

* * *

BEN WAS UP at first light the next morning, and noted with satisfaction that Padilla and his soldiers had already departed. He headed for the stable, then stopped and reached for his knife as movement caught his attention near one of the sheds. His hand dropped away when he spied the slight figure of Pilar in the shadows.

He moved to her and asked, "What are you doin' up so early? Something wrong? You're not hurt or anything, are you?"

Tears rimmed her eyes as Pilar looked up at him and said, "I'm fine. It's not that. I just had to talk to you before you left to apologize for all the trouble I caused."

"No harm done . . ." Ben started, but she interrupted, "It's not all right. I knew you would say that. It was a stupid thing for me to do. You could have been hurt, or even killed, because of the way I acted." Then she paused and batted her eyes before she said, "After all, we hardly even kissed."

Before Ben could answer, Pilar went up on her tip toes, threw her arms around his neck and kissed him full on the mouth. His arms went instinctively around her slender waist and he held her close until she broke off the kiss and stepped back.

Pilar took his hand in hers and said, "You are quite the bravest and most honorable man I have ever met, and I think I am in love with you."

Ben started to reply, but Pilar touched his lips with her fingers and said, "No, don't say anything now. Just think about it while you are gone. We will talk when you return. If you feel the same about me, you will return."

Without another word, Pilar turned and scooted toward the main house. Ben started to go after her, but pulled up short when Paco called out, "*Hermano*, over here. I have something to show you."

He looked around to find Paco and Uncle Ezra at the entrance to the barn.

Ezra had a big grin on his face when he said, "A thing here you need to see, boy."

Ben moved toward the two men, his mind a blur. As he approached, the white stallion Paco rode in the ring was brought out of the barn. Ben looked closer and saw that his saddle, not Paco's, was on the big horse.

He turned toward the *segundo* in confusion.

Paco removed his hat, then with a broad smile on his face, said, "My present to you."

"'Preciate it," Ben stammered, "He's a beautiful animal, but I can't take your horse. You two are as one when you are mounted on him."

Paco laughed and said, "But *señor*, this is *El Caballo Padre Plata*, the silver stallion. He is brother to my own white stud, and since I wish for the two of us to be as brothers, he is now yours."

Ben said, "He's a valuable animal. I have nothin' to give in return."

Paco said solemnly, "At the fiesta, you gave me back my dignity. The horse is small repayment."

Ben took Paco's hand and said, "I'll treasure the silver stallion always . . . brother."

Joseph walked over and said, "It is time for us to leave. The four of us will ride out with one pack horse. If Ramon left a soldier behind, it will look like we are a hunting party. My *vaqueros* will meet us south of here with everything needed for the journey."

A cloud of dust marked the line of march used by Joseph's men, and they caught up with them by mid-morning. The riders drove a herd of mustangs and had several sturdy wagons filled with supplies.

Ben scouted their back trail, but found no sign to indicate they were being followed, then ranged out far ahead of the column to search for a place they could use as a base of operations.

The country around him took on a different tone, became more wild, more rugged. Ben had to change direction several times because of heavy brush and finally was confronted with a thicket so dense he was forced to detour more than a mile to the east before he found a suitable route for the horse herd to pass through. He forded many streams that ran clean and clear over sandy bottoms and passed through places where reeds towered so high above his head they blocked the sun from view.

Ben spotted only a few longhorns, although sign of them being in the area increased as he moved further south and the sound of cattle moving in the brush was all around him. Then a huge longhorn bull charged from Ben's rear as he moved into a small clearing. The brindle color of the animal had made it all but invisible to Ben when he passed.

The silver stallion proved equal to the challenge. It twisted to the left with incredible agility and avoided the horns easily, then turned so fast that had Ben not been securely seated in the saddle, he would have been thrown to the ground. The horse danced to the side, while the bull continued its headlong rush across the clearing and disappeared into the brush.

Ben used his neckerchief to wipe the sweat from his brow and patted the stallion on the neck, then nudged the horse in the ribs and moved slowly forward, more alert now.

Ben found a lake surrounded by a large meadow late in the afternoon and built a fire to guide the others to him. He unsaddled the stallion and had just finished giving the horse a rubdown when they arrived.

Ben watched the *vaqueros* rig a rope corral for the horse herd, then nodded to the men and said, "Coffee's on."

Joseph poured two cups, then handed one to Ben and said, "The countryside is crawling with cattle, my men picked up thirty head along the trail on the way in. Is this the best place for the gather?"

Ben accepted his coffee, then said, "Ought to do. There's two box canyons with water and plenty of grass about a mile to the east. These longhorns don't seem to like to run with each other, 'n I figger it'll be best if we bunch 'em together so they'll get used to the idea before we put 'em on the trail. Might gentle 'em down a bit."

"That is a good plan, *compadre*," Paco said as he walked up. "I have been worried about how we were going to keep the cattle in a group. The most longhorns we have moved at any one time is thirty, and that small number required four of my best men to keep them together. If the cattle are tamed before we start out, they should be easier to handle."

"Judgin' by what I've seen of the critters," Ben said dryly, "We won't get 'em tamed, but we might take a little of the edge off." Then he turned to Joseph and asked, "This about the southern edge of your *rancho*? Didn't find any markers."

"I believe so," Joseph said, then added with pride, "This was the first private land grant awarded in the province of Texas. It was deeded jointly to my grandfather and Don Andres Hernandez on a grant issued by of the King of Spain in 1758. They divided the land among themselves, but it has never been completely surveyed or exact boundary lines established."

Ben thought back to the colonies where he'd seen whole families try to kill each other over a sliver of overworked earth that lay between two properties, ground not nearly as rich and fertile as that in this wild country.

He poked a stick at the sandy soil and asked, "How 'bout your neighbors? They don't get upset if they think you're using land they claim?"

Joseph stood up and swept his arm out at the empty expanse and said, "Out here, Ben, we have an abundance of land, more than we can make use of. One day, I suppose, we will mark our boundaries and maybe even put up fences, but at this time we are not concerned with the movement of others across our land."

"And the cattle, who decides which animals belongs to who?"

"There are so many, it has never been a problem," Joseph said with a smile. "The *ranchos* in Spain put their mark on their animals, they call it a brand, to show ownership, but few here have ever felt the need."

Joseph and Paco left to get the camp set up. Ezra walked over to Ben and said, "Sounds right friendly 'round here, don't it. You studied on where we're gonna take these beeves when we get 'em gathered?"

"Got me a pretty good idea. One of Paco's riders is part Indian, from the Caddo tribe. His people used to live east of here, 'n told him there's a way through. I'll leave in the mornin' to check it out. While I'm gone, keep a sharp lookout for Padilla 'n his soldiers. Could be, we ain't seen the last of that 'pop-in-jay.'"

Ezra rubbed his chin, then said, "Maybe so. If I spot 'em 'n get the chance, think I ought to take him out?"

"Just keep an eye on him, 'n make sure the *vaqueros* stay mostly near the box canyons. If he shows up, we'll handle it when I get back."

Chapter Eleven

BEN ROLLED OUT OF HIS blankets well before daylight the next morning, but found the Mexican cook up before him. Coffee already boiled and beans steamed over the fire.

Ben wolfed down two plates of beans and several cups of scalding coffee, then had the cook pack him grub for ten days.

He saddled his roan instead of the silver stallion because he wanted the big horse rested and ready to go when they started to move the cattle.

The rest of the camp started to come to life as he gave a wave of his hand and rode out to the east. Ben made a wide circle into the hills before he left, but found no indication that the activity below was being observed.

Ben found the going easy for the first two days with plenty of grass for the cattle and many streams that would afford water for the herd. Game was abundant and he found no sign of recent Indian activity.

The ground under his horse started to gently rise at mid-morning of the third day, then became broken and rocky. He was forced to move in and out of the craggy terrain until he reached the top of a steep mountain. Ben scouted along the edge of the plateau, and finally he spotted a way, far below, for them to get the cattle through if they drove them around the southern base of the peak.

Ben eased his way down the eastern slope toward the valley and could see several more ridges ahead that would have to be negotiated. Halfway to the bottom, movement at the edge of the trees caught his eye and he reined in behind some boulders.

Ben pulled out his spyglass and focused on the shadows until he made out the figures of an Indian man and woman. He studied the pair. The squaw led pack animals and the two riders seemed to be alone. The brave was big for an Indian and well armed with two rifles strapped to his horse, but not painted for war. Ben watched the small party move out of sight, then swept the rest of the valley with his glass.

He waited for half an hour, then decided it was safe to move out and left the boulders with his gun at the ready.

Ben scratched his head and wondered why the brave was here with his squaw. An Indian hunting alone wasn't unusual, but they never took their women with them, then he decided it wasn't his concern and picked his way through the rocks to the bottom of the hill.

He stayed along the edge of the trees and moved around the valley in the opposite direction of that taken by the Indians. Ben made it to the ridge on the other side without incident and started up the incline, then motion in the valley behind him caught his eye.

Ben eased in behind some trees and witnessed a sight in the valley so beautiful it made him catch his breath. He watched as first a few, then more than a hundred wild mustangs wandered out of the trees and started to graze on the lush grass of the meadow below. The horses were fat, their coats sleek and shiny in the summer sun, mostly mares, with a few colts that frolicked around the edges.

He scanned the surrounding area for the leader of the herd. The dominant stallion was the one that defeated all other male horses in battle and by doing so earned the right to rule and have first choice of the mares. This method of selective breeding insured the blood line of the herd would remain strong and give the horses the best chance to survive.

Ben had about given up when a magnificent black appeared on a rocky ledge a hundred feet below him. Muscles rippled under the stallion's skin as he nervously stamped his hoofs on the rock while he surveyed his charges below, ever on the alert to warn them of danger.

He grinned to himself and thought, with this horse as the stud, the blood line of the herd below was in good shape. After a moment more, Ben eased back and slanted up the hill to the north. When nearly to the top, he came to a steep ravine that cut through the face of the mountain. Ben smiled in satisfaction when he worked his way down to the bottom and found the ravine widened and flattened out. If it didn't come to a dead end, this would be the way to get the cattle to the other side of the mountain.

Ben was edgy. He had that itchy feeling between his shoulders that someone was watched him, maybe even stalked him. Ben stopped to take a sip from his canteen, then splashed water on his face and poured some in his hat so his horse could drink. Something moved in the bushes above and behind him, but when he looked, nothing was there.

He checked to make sure his pistols were primed, then moved into the shadow of the south wall and walked his horse east along the floor of the ravine.

Suddenly, Ben heard the growl of a mountain cat above him. He threw his rifle to his shoulder, but found no target. Then he heard a gunshot, followed by a loud crash and the snarling of a lion locked in battle.

Ben left the saddle and clawed his way up the side of the gully toward the sound. Halfway to the top, he moved around a jumble of boulders and was momentarily stunned by what he saw. A dead mustang lay on the ground twenty yards from Ben with an Indian pinned beneath the animal who frantically tried to fight off the attack of a mountain lion with only a small hand axe. The muscles in the brave's back and neck rippled and swelled with the effort, but blood was all around him and he was growing weaker by the second.

Ben raised his rifle to his shoulder and fired. Through the smoke of the blast, he saw his ball strike the big cat full in the head and the lion's skull explode.

He reloaded his weapon and moved forward with it at the ready. The Indian's impassive black eyes stared at Ben as he walked up, then closed with a flutter as the brave fell back in a faint.

Ben checked and found the man was alive, then recognized him as the one he saw with his squaw in the valley. He freed the Indian's leg from under the pony, then carried him to the floor of the ravine. He examined the brave's wounds and found them not to be life threatening, then dressed the torn flesh and laid the man on a blanket. Ben covered the wounded brave, then returned to the dead mustang to retrieve the Indian's weapons and placed them near the unconscious man.

Shadows were long in the ravine, so Ben picketed his horse before he built a fire and put a coffee pot in the coals, then started to mix up something to eat. Ben watched out of the corner of his eye as he stirred the beans, but took no action when the Indian moved, first his hand, then tried to sit up.

Ben turned from the fire when the brave fell weakly back to the blanket and asked, "Are you hungry? *Tienen hambre?*"

The Indian slowly lifted his head and glanced, first at the fresh bandages, then at his weapons beside him on the ground. Finally, he faced Ben and replied in surprisingly good English, "I am called Hacha, and would eat, if you have enough."

Ben fixed a plate and handed it over, then dished one up for himself and said, "Name's Ben Cross. I saw you today in the valley, you and a woman, headin' south. How do you come to be in this place?"

"I see the sun flash from your glass and follow."

"Why come after me? I was goin' away from you and the woman. You plan to kill me, did ya?"

"Hacha have chance to kill, but not take. These mountains are home to me. No white men come here. When I see you, I want to know why you are here."

Ben nodded his head. He knew what the Indian said about being able to kill him was probably true, then he said, "I mean you no harm. I'm here to find a way to drive a herd of cattle through the mountains. We won't stay, just pass through."

"It matters not that you stay or go," Hacha said, as he struggled to sit up. "Once a trail is found, others will come."

Ben helped him, then said, "Your wounds are not serious, but you lost a lot of blood. How'd that lion get the jump on you, anyway?"

"There were two of the mountain cats. I shot one, then lost my musket when the mate killed my horse. My woman has my other gun, and the lion was about to send me to meet the Great Spirit when you killed it. I owe you my life."

"Speakin' of your woman. Where's she now?"

"I hear noise in the trees behind you, Ben Cross, and I think my woman is there with a gun aimed at you."

The muscles in Ben's back tightened. He hadn't heard any noise, then Hacha called out, "Paloma, come. This man is a friend."

Ben turned to see the lithe figure of a young Indian woman materialize from the darkness. The barrel of the weapon in her hands never wavered from Ben's chest. The girl walked slowly into the light, and he saw she was lovely. Her jet black hair framed a finely etched face and her pale white, beaded, doe-skin dress outlined a trim, compact figure.

She walked to the wounded man and asked, "Why do you say this man is friend? You are his prisoner and still bleed."

"Silence woman," Hacha said harshly. "A mountain cat would have killed me if not for this man. I owe him my life. I am not a prisoner. My weapons are beside me. The wounds are scratches."

Ben was seemingly forgotten as the girl lay the musket down and checked Hacha's bandages. After a few minutes, she looked at Ben and said, "I thank you for what you do for my man. What is on cuts?"

"Mixture o' bear fat and gunpowder."

She nodded her head in agreement with the treatment, then said, "I am Paloma. I will get my horse."

He watched her move in the darkness, then turned to Hacha and said, "You have a strong woman."

A smile seemed to touch Hacha's lips when he said, "Paloma is a good woman. At times, too strong, maybe."

BEN WAS AMAZED when he looked at Hacha over breakfast the next morning. The night's rest, and the food he wolfed down, had restored most of the strength the Indian lost in his encounter with the lion.

"You look well this morning," Ben said.

"My wounds heal. Your medicine is strong."

"How is it you speak English? You didn't learn here in the mountains."

Hacha thought for a moment, then said, "I am Yaqui. Paloma is Apache. Our tribes war with each other. She was taken prisoner when a child. I want her as my woman when she grows up, but it is forbidden by the laws of my tribe. I steal Paloma and we go to the Spanish mission at *Ysleta*, near *El Paso del Norte*. The *Padre* at the church teach us English and Spanish."

"Why'd you leave the mission?"

Hacha looked up and his black eyes flashed sparks as he said passionately, "Three soldiers get drunk and attack

Paloma on way to our cabin. I kill them and we come to mountains. Now this is our home."

Ben studied the man in front of him and decided it was a good thing Hacha had not wanted him dead yesterday. "I search for a way to move cattle through the mountains. Do you know of such a place, and about the land toward the rising sun from here?"

Hacha appeared puzzled and asked, "Why you want cattle on other side mountain? No white men live there."

Ben looked at the Yaqui, not sure how to explain. He knew the average Indian's idea of war was to raid a village, then return to his home to celebrate the victory and wouldn't understand the way the white man would fight for years to settle a single conflict. He finally said, "It's a long story. Far to the east, my people are in a struggle for freedom with our mother country, England. We have friends from Spain that would help us, but they have no food for their soldiers. It's my job to get the Spanish a supply of meat so they can go to war and help us defeat our enemies."

"But, you are English. You fight your own people?"

Ben shrugged his shoulders and said, "We're the same, but different. Like the Apache and the Yaqui. We are no longer English. We are Americans, born here and want the right to rule ourselves."

Hacha nodded his head as if he understood, then asked, "Cattle you bring same as the *Padre* had at mission?"

"Doubt it. Those were tame. We're roundin' up wild un's that run free in the brush."

Hacha's eyes widened and his mouth dropped open, then he recovered and said, "You wish to take the loco ones with the long horns through the mountains," then he shook his from side to side and added, "They will not go."

"Still, it's a thing that must be done. Those cows are the only supply of meat there is. The Spanish might be our best chance to defeat the English, so I plan to get 'em to

New Orleans so Governor Galvez can mount his attack. I could use your help."

Hacha picked up a stick and drew a crude map in the sand, then said, "We are here. This ravine comes out on the other side, then you can go around hills to flat country. No more mountains."

"What 'bout the rivers? You know of a place where we can get cattle across?"

"Maybe so. I go with Paloma to cabin and get horse. Hacha meet you on other side of mountains, then we see."

Chapter Twelve

BEN CLIMBED TO THE TOP of the mountain near the mouth of the ravine and surveyed the country to the east while he waited for Hacha to arrive. He could see that driving the cattle through the rolling hills would present no problem and the land on the other side leveled out into a vast sea of grass, with only small patches of the heavy mesquite briars and thorny brush that caused riders so much trouble where the longhorns were being gathered.

Being able to keep the cattle bunched in the confines of the passes and ravines through the mountains for the first few days might make the longhorns more manageable. Not having to contend with the thick spiny overgrowth of briars would definitely make the *vaquero's* job easier once the cattle made it out of the hills.

Hacha arrived at mid-morning on a blaze-faced sorrel mare that stood as tall as the roan ridden by Ben.

Ben raised his hand in greeting when the Indian rode up, then offered Hacha a canteen and said, "It warms my heart you have come."

The Yaqui accepted a drink and said, "I said I'd be here," then kicked his horse in the ribs and led the way into the hills with Ben close behind.

The two men rode slowly through the rolling country-side. Ben noticed, even though lush grass covered the ground, a cloud of dust was kicked up by the hooves of their horses and the grass crackled and broke as they passed over it.

Ben reined in close beside his companion and said, "Land 'round here is thirsty. We gonna have any trouble finding water for the cattle?"

Hacha waved his hand toward the east and replied, "Plenty of streams and rivers. I will show. Not rain here for long time, but will soon."

"How do you know the rain is comin'?"

"It is time," Hacha said simply.

Ben studied on the answer for a moment, then asked, "What about the Indians that live here? Will they fight to keep us from goin' through their land?"

Hacha spat on the ground, then said with contempt, "This is home to the Caddoes, digger Indians. They not fight."

Ben thought about the fierce *vaquero* back in camp that said he was of the Caddo tribe and hoped the ones they met wouldn't be like him, then he asked, "What about the Comanches? They ever roam this far t' the south?"

"Their land is where the sun leaves the sky. Never see them here, but they not stay long one place, so who can say."

The wind dropped to the point that the tops of the grass hardly moved and the heat became oppressive around them when they left the hills and rode out onto the open plain. They crossed several streams during the day. None of them were dry, but the only really good supply of water was at one fed by a natural spring.

The two men rode in silence as darkness settled over the plain and finally gave them relief from the heat of the day. The light of the full moon allowed them travel late into the night, then they camped in a grove of oak trees.

Ben's mind wandered to thoughts of Pilar before he closed his eyes and he tried to understand what was going on between the two of them. The only thing he knew was, he'd never felt for anyone the way he felt for Pilar. There was Uncle Ezra, of course. Ben wasn't all that sure what love was. He'd noticed the way Hacha and Paloma acted when they were together, and even though Indians were not supposed to show their emotions, it was obvious to him they cared a great deal for each other. The last thing Ben thought before he fell asleep was that caring about someone must have a lot to do with love.

Hacha shook Ben awake the next morning and handed him a cup of coffee, then pointed to the east and said, "Something on fire."

Ben climbed out of his blankets and saw several spirals of dark smoke visible against the rising sun.

He turned to Hacha and said, "That's a lot of smoke. What's over there?"

"A Spanish settlement, *Villa de Bucareli*, is that way."

"How far away, fifteen . . . twenty miles?"

Hacha nodded his head and Ben continued, "Let's eat some grub, 'n then we'll go check it out. Can we get close without bein' seen?"

"I know of a way," came the reply.

THE SUN WAS high in the sky by the time they stopped in the trees that overlooked the village. Ben dismounted, then used his looking glass to carefully survey the scene below. The fires in the buildings were burned low and little remained except for the adobe brick walls, but he saw no danger.

He handed the glass to Hacha and showed him how to use it, then said, "Nothing moves down there. What do you think?"

The Yaqui peered through the glass, obviously pleased by its magnifying qualities, then returned it to Ben and said, "I think those who do the burning are gone. I go make sure."

Ben touched Hacha on the arm and said, "Circle to the left. I'll go right. Travel with care."

Ben moved carefully down the slope on foot, and it was thirty minutes before he rested against the wall of the southern most building. Sweat stained Ben's shirt and it stuck to his back as he pulled back the hammer of his rifle to check the priming, then eased to the corner and peered around at the center of the small town.

Ben spotted no movement of any kind in the dusty street, then relaxed and lowered his weapon when Hacha stepped into the open two doors away and signaled for Ben to come.

He hurried to the Yaqui's side and asked, "What'd you find?"

The Indian looked puzzled as he said, "Nothing here. No people, no bodies, not even a dog or fresh grave."

"Got to be somethin'. Somebody burned the town," Ben said, then both men tensed at a strange scraping sound that came from behind one of the buildings.

Neither man spoke. They just looked at each other, then separated and went to investigate.

Ben moved around the east side of a burned out building, then stopped and stared at what he saw. An elderly Spanish man was propped up against the back wall. The man's naked body was covered with gore and a trail of blood marked where he'd drug himself into the shade.

The man appeared lifeless, then Ben saw the Spaniard's foot twitch against a rain barrel and make the sound they heard from the street.

Hacha stood to the side while Ben knelt and used a wet rag to wipe some of the blood from the injured man's face.

The old one's eyes flickered open for an instant, then slowly closed and Ben asked, "Can you understand me, old one? *Habla ustéd Ingles*? Do you speak English?"

Ben received no response and glanced up at Hacha, then looked quickly back down when a weak voice murmured, "*Si*, I speak the *Inglés*."

Ben washed the ancient one's forehead and asked, "How are you called, *Tio*?"

"Sebastian Diaz," came the reply as the eyes slowly opened. Then he said, "I have a thirst."

Ben looked down where the man's stomach was split wide open and his intestines trailed in the dirt. The water wouldn't do him any good, but it couldn't do him any harm either, so Ben lifted the canteen to Sebastian's lips, then asked, "Can you tell us what happened here? Where everybody is?"

The water caused the old man to choke at first, but seemed to ease his pain for the moment, and he said, "The people of *Villa de Bucareri* are all gone, two weeks, now. The Indians kill those who go to work in fields, then river take part of the village after storehouse of winter food burn and *Capitán* Gil Ybarbo decide this place is bad and everyone must go back to settle again in the north."

Ben, amazed Sebastian was still alive and knowing the man could not last much longer, asked, "Why'd they leave you behind?"

"My wife, my Rosa is here. She rests with the Angels in the hallowed ground behind the mission. I could not leave her. The people left, but I stay behind to live out my days with her. The Comanches find me when I talk with my Rosa. They leave me when they grow tired of the tormenting." Then Sebastian seized Ben's arm with a surprisingly strong grip and said, "Give me your word that you will place me at rest beside my beloved wife before you go."

"Take it easy, old timer. I'll do as you wish. How many Indians in the bunch that got you, 'n when did they leave?"

"Many Comanches, *señor*, many . . . more than I can count. They leave today . . . yesterday . . . I not know."

The old man slumped back and his eyes closed for the last time as he murmured, "Remember your promise."

Ben placed his fingers at the base of Sebastian's neck, but life had flown from the old Spaniard's body.

Hacha motioned with his gun and said, "We go now. Too long in this place."

Ben rose slowly to his feet, then pointed at the dead man and said, "Soon's we put him in the ground with his wife."

Hacha shook his head, then said, "No good to bury. Comanches maybe come back to torture him some more. If he not here, they will come after us. Besides, we have no way to dig."

Ben thought for a moment, then told Hacha, "Help me drag him to his wife's grave. When the Indians come back, they'll figger he crawled there to die."

They lay Sebastian on his stomach with his arms outstretched around the mound of earth that held his wife. Ben thought the trail of blood to the grave was convincing.

He stood back and removed his cap, then said, "Best I can do to keep my word, old timer. Least you're restin' along side your Rosa. I'll do a proper job when I get back."

Ben put on his hat, then turned to Hacha and said, "I'll get rid of our sign in the village. You circle 'round and see which way the Comanches went. Meet ya where we left the horses."

Hacha studied Ben's face for a long minute, then gave a nod of his head and started for the north end of town.

Ben used a piece of brush to wipe their footprints from the sand and made sure to stay on grass or rock while he worked his way back up the hill.

He tightened the cinch on his horse and was ready to go when the Yaqui arrived.

Hachi held up a headband and said, "They were Comanches. Fifty, sixty riders, many horses. They leave that way, back where we come from."

Ben scratched his chin before he asked, "You figger war party or could they just be on a hunt?"

"With Comanches, it is always war."

"Why would they go west toward the hills? You said they didn't even travel down here on the plains, much less in the mountains."

Hacha gave a shrug and said simply, "They are Comanches."

"The Indians'll have to wait. We still got to find a way to get the cattle to Louisiana."

They rode hard to the east, and the only Indian sign they ran across was a few tracks that Hacha said belonged to hunters from a Caddoe village to the north.

Hacha led Ben to the top of a ridge that overlooked the Sabine River late in the afternoon of the next day. The light that reflected from the gently rolling water reminded them how hot and dusty they were. The sun had beat down on them for days, without even the hint of a cloud in the sky.

Hacha waved his arm and said, "This is the place I tell of. Water is low, bottom hard for long way."

Ben removed the pistol belt from around his waist and placed it on his saddle horn, then gigged the roan in the ribs and left the hill at a run. He galloped his horse to the middle the river, then pulled up and left the back of the stallion in a flying leap in the water, clothes and all. He came to the surface with a whoop, then sat in the mud of the bottom and let the river soak the strain from his weary muscles.

Hacha followed him in and the two of them splashed around in the water like kids. After they were both thoroughly soaked and relaxed, Ben led the way out onto a sand bar so the sun could dry them off.

The river was well below bank level, so Ben mounted and walked his horse into the water and splashed out on the other side, then guided the roan back and forth across the river for a hundred yards in both directions from where he first entered and found the bottom sound all the way.

He came out of the water and moved to where Hacha waited in a grove of trees, then extended his hand and said, "You were right, partner. Cattle'll be able to ford the river here.

Hacha accepted Ben's hand, then said, "Trail is no problem, if long horn cows will come."

Ben smiled grimly and said, "We'll get 'em here, but without your help, I couldn't a found the trail or a way across the river this fast. Any debt owed to me is paid in full, 'n you're free to leave. Hacha, the Yaqui, will always be in the heart of Ben Cross."

Hacha didn't say anything for a moment, then asked, "Where you go now?"

"I'm gonna backtrack those Comanches, 'n see if they're gonna cause us any trouble."

The Yaqui placed his fist over his heart and stated, "Hacha come too. See his friend stay safe."

"I'd like that," Ben said with a grin, then they mounted and rode to the west.

Chapter Thirteen

THEY PUSHED HARD AND THE shadows were long on the ground by the time they reined in their lathered mounts near the still smoldering remains of *Villa de Bucareli* the next day. Hacha led Ben to the west side of town where they picked up the tracks of the Comanches.

The trail left by the departed braves was still clear. Hacha soon turned into a gully where the Indians had made camp and handed the reins of his horse to Ben while he moved around the edge of the campsite with his eyes on the ground.

Ben looked up at the sky to see dark clouds had started to build in the north and the smell of moisture was in the air.

He slid off of his horse, then went to Hacha and said, "Storm's comin'. Looks like a big'n too. Rain hits tonight, them Indians tracks'll be gone come mornin'."

Hacha finished his examination, then turned to Ben and said, "It will not matter if storm comes."

"What'd you mean, don't matter? Course it does. We got no chance to follow the Comanches without a trail."

"They split up here. Small bands go all different ways. Main bunch go toward mountain ahead. We go that way too."

Ben checked the sign for himself, then stood up and said, "Don't like it. No reason for 'em to send out more 'n a few braves if they were huntin' meat. We better watch our backside, they could circle around 'n surprise us. Got any idea what they're doin'?"

Hacha shrugged his shoulders, then said, "This land is new to them. Maybe they send out scouts to see what is here."

Their eyes swept the horizon as they mounted and headed out. The Comanches next campsite was located only a short distance from the first and tracks of the arrival and departure of small groups of riders marked the ground around it.

Ben noticed the wind start to freshen as he studied the sign and straightened up to say, "Still headin' the same way. Weather's gonna turn sour pretty quick—we better find us somewhere to ride out the storm."

"We go to a cave near here."

Ben nodded his head and said, "Lead the way. Feel better if I knew where them Comanches was headin', but there's no help for it now."

Hacha looked at Ben and said, "You not worry. We will get to mountain first. Find their camp tomorrow."

Heavy weather descended around them as they arrived at the cave. First came the rain, followed by heavy hail, some of it the size of pigeon eggs.

The icy balls covered the ground behind them as they guided their mounts through the large entrance of the cave, and Ben noted it widened into a huge cavern once they were inside.

They unsaddled their horses and rubbed them down with grass, then Ben used some dry branches he found in the back to build a fire. The wood was neatly stacked, as if someone left it there and planned to return.

He turned to Hacha and asked, "You leave the wood here?"

"Same ones who leave wood, do that," Hacha said, as he waved his arm toward the rocky sides of the enclosure where the light from the fire revealed crude scenes and figures painted on the walls.

Ben pointed at the drawings and said, "What are these, 'n how'd they get here?"

"The ancient ones put them there," Hacha replied.

"Who're you talkin' about?"

Hacha squatted down and said, "Many pictures like these in caves to the south where my people live. The wise men of my tribe say ancestors of Yaqui make signs. People who are dead for long time."

Ben studied the drawings on the wall, scenes of men hunting and of warriors locked in battle. Others portrayed groups of people—men, women, and children who worked and played outside a cave such as the one here. The weapons the men in the scenes used were crude. No guns or even a bow, only short spears with sharpened ends.

He and Ezra had found similar scenes on the walls of a cave high in the Allegheny mountains and Ben wondered if there was a connection.

He wished he knew more about those who painted the scenes and how long ago they roamed this land. The pictures could be the history of an entire people.

Ben returned to the fire and stared through the flames at Hacha. The Yaqui didn't have to be here. He could be back home with his woman, but Ben felt a strong kinship for Hacha and was glad the Indian chose to be with him. To get the cattle to New Orleans wasn't going to be easy and Ben wanted the Yaqui at his side if trouble came.

Rain and hail still pelted the rocks outside the cave when they went to sleep that night, but when they rolled out of their blankets in the pre-dawn hours the next day the ground was wet from the storm, but the ice was all gone.

They led their horses out of the cave after breakfast, pulled the cinches tight on their saddles and prepared to leave. The rain had stopped, but the day was overcast and gloomy, and clouds would hide the sun when it came up.

Ben climbed in the saddle and said, "We'll split up and see if we can locate the Comanches. Meet back here at noon, whether you've found 'em or not. Time for me to get back to the cattle 'n I want a talk to you 'fore I go."

Ben circled to the east. Not knowing where the Indians were, he had to stay under cover and move with care. He crossed the tracks of two small groups of riders, and was forced to wait almost an hour in a grove of oak trees for five painted warriors to pass his place of concealment.

He turned back toward the cave at mid-morning without any sign of the main band of Comanches. Hacha already had a small smokeless fire going with coffee and beans on when he arrived.

The Yaqui handed Ben a cup and said, "I find their camp in next valley. Not look good."

Ben took a sip of the steaming liquid and asked, "What's that mean?"

"Braves build wickiups, hang meat to dry. They would not do that if they do not plan to stay."

Ben scratched his chin and said, "Don't make no sense. Braves I saw were painted for war. Indians on the warpath don't stop and make camp. What do you make of it?"

Hacha slowly shook his head, then said, "No way to know for sure. Maybe they plan to move rest of village here, or they could change mind and leave soon."

"Is the camp close to where we'll be drivin' the cattle?"

"Not far."

"Then we've got to hope they move before we get back, or we'll be in for a fight."

"Makes no difference to me. First you come, now Comanches. Not safe now. I must get Paloma and leave."

Ben reached across and placed his hand on Hacha's shoulder and asked, "You want to go with me? Help me get the cattle through? You can take Paloma?"

"Would that I could, but it can not be."

"Why? Don't know how much we can pay, but I'll make sure you get somethin'."

"Pay does not matter. It is the soldiers I killed at *Ysleta*. The Spanish would put me to death for that."

Ben thought for a moment, then said, "The leader of the

soldiers with cattle is my friend. I think I can square things for you. 'Til I do, you stay out of sight. Scout ahead 'n report only to me. I won't let any harm come to you, or Paloma. That, I promise you."

Hacha thought for a moment, then said simply, "I will come."

Ben smiled and said, "Good. I'll head on back. Get Paloma and meet me in the trees above the box canyons I told you about."

Hacha said, "I know the place," then leaped on his horse and, with a wave of his hand, galloped off in a cloud of dust.

Ben watched Hacha ride off, then mounted and started up the hill to get a look at the Comanche camp before he left.

The sun was still high in the sky when Ben eased into position above the Indian encampment and found things pretty much the way Hacha described them. Fifteen or twenty braves worked in the camp. They erected wickiups, stacked firewood, and dressed out game. He wasn't as worried about the Indians he saw below as he was about the ones that weren't there. Ben just hoped the scouting parties didn't wander far enough to find out where the cattle were being gathered. He took one final look, then made his way back to his horse and headed down the valley to the ravine where they'd bring the cattle through.

Ben rode hard and once out of the mountains found no sign that the Comanches had come this far. He traveled all night and stopped only to give his horse a chance to blow. By noon of the next day he was near the place he'd left Uncle Ezra and the others.

Ben moved in position above the mouth of the first box canyon and looked down to find the valley below brimming with longhorns. He watched two *vaqueros* come into sight as they rode around the cattle to keep the animals calm. Then Ben's eyes narrowed. The *vaqueros* were unarmed. Not a musket on either horse and no pistol or even a knife in their belts.

Ben took out his spyglass and carefully inspected the area, then muttered, "Damn," when he finally spotted a campfire in the shade of some trees. Around the fire were three heavily armed soldiers in Spanish uniforms, all strangers to him.

He pulled back from the edge, then took his horse and made a wide detour around the second canyon. Ben circled the lake until he was down wind from the camp. He left his horse tied to a limb and crawled through the trees until he had clear view into the clearing.

The *vaqueros* were all seated in the shade around the two wagons, even though it was still the middle of the afternoon. Uncle Ezra was there too, along with Sergeant Garcia and the others under Joseph's command. None of the men around the wagons had weapons, except, that is, for the four Spanish soldiers who stood guard. Other armed men in uniform were scattered around the camp. Ben counted eight more guards, but he didn't see the *segundo*, Paco Ruiz, or Joseph anywhere.

Joseph walked out from behind the wagon and beside him was the strutting figure of Ramon Padilla. The two men were having a heated discussion, then Joseph threw down his cigar in disgust and walked away.

The whole thing started to make sense to Ben. Somehow Padilla had found out about the cattle drive and taken over the camp. Problem was, Ben didn't know how he was going to get it back without being forced to kill Padilla and the soldiers. He decided to wait until night and try to get a chance to talk to one of the prisoners.

The soldiers seemed to relax as darkness settled over the camp and Ben was able to work his way through the trees to the edge of the clearing, only twenty feet or so from where Uncle Ezra was seated.

Ben picked up some acorns and, when the guard walked to the other end of the wagon, threw one and hit his uncle in the back of the neck.

Ezra didn't make any sudden moves, instead he slowly turned until he faced toward the trees.

Ben checked the position of the guards when his uncle was all the way around, then stepped into the open for an instant. He saw Ezra give a slight nod of his head and moved quickly back into the shadows to kneel behind some bushes.

Ezra turned his back to the trees, then called the closest guard over and asked, "Okay for me to go out in the woods for a minute?"

The guard asked, "For what purpose, *señor?*"

"What'd you mean, for what purpose, you blitherin' idiot? I got t' go make water, that's what for. I'm an old man, 'n my kidneys ain't what they once was."

The guard looked embarrassed and said, "It is permitted, but I warn you to stay where you can be seen."

Ezra walked slowly into the woods and began to relieve himself beside the bushes where Ben hid.

Ben whispered, "What'n hell happened here, Uncle Ezra?"

"My fault, boy. Let 'em surprise us, I did. That there Padilla, heard somethin' at the fiesta, 'n followed us. Jumped us yesterday. Picked up our riders, one by one, out in the bush, then surrounded the camp and took over. We never had a chance. Sorry 'bout that, boy."

"No time for that now. How many soldier boys Padilla have?"

"Twenty, I counted 'em. Some at the box canyons, rest of 'em scattered 'round here."

Ben thought for a moment, then slipped Uncle Ezra a pistol and two knives and said, "Arm Sergeant Gomez and one other."

He was interrupted by the guard calling out, "Enough, old one. Come back with the others."

Ezra slid the weapons under his deerskin blouse and said, "Be through in a minute, damn your hide. Takes me a little while."

Ben said, "Pass the word to the rest of the men to be ready. I got some help out here, or will have. We'll take the soldiers in the canyons first. Don't worry, I'll be back."

"Another thing you need to know, boy."

Ben looked up at his uncle and asked, "What's that?"

"Pilar's here. She 'n *Doña* Maria come up with a driver a couple days ago. Women 'r over in that tent."

"Pilar. . . here? What'n hell's she doin' here?" Ben paused, then said, "No matter. We're gonna try'n take the guards with no shootin'. If a ruckus starts, your job's to see to her."

Ezra nodded his head and Ben faded back into the trees.

Chapter Fourteen

BEN RETRIEVED HIS HORSE AND circled wide around camp, then headed for the trees above the box canyon where he was to meet Hacha and Paloma. He formed a rough idea in his head as he rode, but they'd need to make plans if the three of them were going to get the cattle back.

Hacha's camp was well back in the heavy thicket and Ben would have gone right by the little gully if his nose hadn't detected the odor of venison simmering over a fire. He tied his horse and moved silently to the edge of the camp where he found Paloma alone. Ben stepped out of the trees with his hands out from his side, and said, "Smells mighty good. Your man around?"

Paloma turned, then from only a few feet behind Ben the voice of Hacha said, "I am here."

Ben greeted the Yaqui with a grin and said, "You move like the wind, my friend. Glad you're here. See any Comanches on the way?"

Hacha smiled at the compliment, then said, "No sign after we leave mountains. Much on the other side."

"We'll handle 'em when we get there. Right now we got other problems," Ben said slowly.

He told Hacha about the situation at the cattle camp, then said, "Don't want any of the guards killed if we can avoid it. I figger to capture the soldiers at the box canyons first—shouldn't be more'n three or four in each place

We'll arm the *vaqueros* who are with the cattle and take the main camp."

Hacha said, "These men are your enemies. Be easy for us if we kill."

"You're right. Makes it harder this way, but if we kill the soldiers, every Spaniard in Texas will be out to stop us, n' our job is still to get the cattle through."

Hacha nodded his head to say he understood, then said, "Plan is good. We eat first, then go."

Ben had nothing to eat but jerky in over a day, so he said, "Sounds good to me."

THE MOON WAS high overhead, peeking through the clouds, by the time they were in position at the first canyon. The longhorns were bedded down and two *vaqueros* moved around the outskirts of the cattle.

Hacha scouted ahead and reported four soldiers at the campfire, none of them very alert, and only *vaqueros* were with the herd.

Ben whispered to Hacha, "Work 'round to the other side of the fire. Signal me when you're in place, 'n I'll step out into the clearing. If you have to shoot, use your bow and try to wound."

Hacha said, "I will take Paloma."

"No need to put your woman in danger. Leave her here."

Hacha shrugged his shoulders and said simply, "She will help." Then the two of them vanished into the dark.

Ben studied the four men around the fire while he waited. One of them walked to the edge of the trees in front of Ben, and when the hoot of an owl sounded from across the clearing, Ben stepped into the open and clubbed the soldier over the head, then walked forward with his brace of pistols leveled at the other men and said, "*Alto*, no *movimiento*."

Hacha and Paloma moved in behind the soldiers to disarm them before the men had a chance to react.

The prisoners were tied up and their weapons gathered by the fire. The whole thing didn't take more than five minutes from start to finish.

The two *vaqueros* rode up and one said, *Señor* Ben, it is good you are back. You are familiar with what happens here?"

"Most of it. You boys help yourselves to them weapons over there. We're gonna take the camp back." Then he said, "This's my friend, Hacha, and his woman, Paloma."

The *vaqueros* looked at each other, then one said, "But, *Señor* Ben, they are Indians."

Ben glared at the men and growled, "They're my friends."

Both vaqueros lowered their heads and the one who had spoken said, "*Si señor*, it is understood."

The matter put out of his mind, Ben checked to see that the four captured men were securely bound, then said, "Hacha, scout the other canyon. Want to be at the main camp 'fore the sun comes up."

Ben led the way and when the small band neared the second box canyon, Hacha rode up to them and reported, "Two soldiers at fire. Two more ride with men who work cattle."

Ben puzzled things over in his mind for a minute, then asked, "How far is it from the fire to where the longhorns are bedded down?"

"Long way."

Ben turned to the *vaqueros* and said, "Let me have those *serape* things you're wearin', your *sombreros* too."

He slipped a *serape* over his shoulders, placed a *sombrero* on his head, then handed the other set to Hacha and said, "Put this on, tuck your hair up under the hat. You 'n me are gonna ride in there like we was *vaqueros* comin' to take the place of those with the cows. We'll go straight to the cattle 'n see if we can get close enough to get the drop on the soldiers."

Ben turned to the others and said, "You three sneak up close to the fire 'n give us cover if we're discovered. We'll get there 'n help with those two, soon's we can."

Ben waited until the moon was hidden behind the clouds, then he and Hacha slowly walked their horses into the canyon. They stayed in the shadows and were well past the men at the fire before the moon reappeared.

They were almost to the cattle when the shadowy figure of a man on a horse appeared out of the gloom. Ben could tell the rider was a soldier by the outline of the peaked hat the man wore, so he pulled the *sombrero* low over his face and gigged his horse in the ribs.

The soldier reined in his horse, but before he could speak, Ben closed with the man, stuck his pistol in the rider's face and said, "*Silencio*."

Hacha pulled the soldier to the ground, then bound and gagged the man and stayed with him while Ben moved around the edge of the bunched cattle.

Ben tensed when a second rider rode toward him, then relaxed as he picked up the outline of a *sombrero* on the man's head. Ben walked his horse up to the man and grinned when he picked out the troubled face of Paco Ruiz in the moonlight.

Ben tipped back his hat and whispered, "*Hola*! brother."

Paco's mouth dropped open. He first smiled, then frowned and stammered, "What . . . ah . . . how . . . ah?"

Ben gripped the *segundo's* forearm to silence his chatter, then said, "Go into all that later. Help me get the other guard."

The last soldier with the cattle was born and raised at Joseph's *Rancho*, and the young man readily surrendered his weapon when ordered to do so by Paco.

Ben led the way back to Hacha and the other soldier, then the last *vaquero* arrived as Ben finished binding the young guard.

Paco gave the Indian a hard look when he rode up, but said nothing.

Ben gathered the men around him and said, "First, we'll get the other two here, then make plans on how to take back the camp from Padilla."

They split up and approached the campfire from two sides. Ben stopped at the edge of the trees, a worried look on his face. Something was wrong. There was no sign of Paloma or the two *vaqueros* with her, and the two soldiers in the clearing appeared to be asleep, then he got a better view and a big grin spread across his face. The two guards weren't moving because they were bound and gagged.

He stepped into the open and called out, "It's all right. Everybody come over here by the fire."

Paco grabbed Ben by the shoulders and said, "It is good to see you, *hermano*. We were beginning to lose hope, but who are these people with you and why do they help us?"

Ben made introductions all around and explained what had happened so far, then he sent Hacha to scout the camp and said, "Uncle Ezra told me Padilla had twenty men with him. We got eight of 'em. That leaves twelve, plus Padilla—we're only seven. We're gonna have to narrow the odds some to take 'em without bloodshed."

He squatted down to draw a crude map in the sand, then pointed at it and said, "This here's a layout o' the camp. Four guards are with our men around the wagons. Uncle Ezra and two of our men are armed, so they'll help us there. The rest o' the soldiers are scattered in the clearing. Some of 'em should be asleep. We'll meet Hacha the other side o' the lake 'n find out where the sentries are posted. Paco, you 'n your *vaqueros*'ll come in from the north. Hacha, Paloma, 'n me'll be on the south side. We'll take out the sentries just before first light. When you hear an owl hoot three times, move into camp. Remember, don't kill if you can help it."

The men nodded they understood, then mounted to follow Ben around the lake.

Paco reined in beside Ben and said, "There is a thing you must know. Pilar is at the camp. She could be hurt if we meet any resistance."

"Uncle Ezra told me, but if we do our job right, there won't be any shootin'."

Hacha met them with the final details and by an hour before daylight everyone was in place.

Ben's eyes strained through the gloom, but the outline of the sentry on the other side of camp wasn't clear, so he'd have to trust Paco to do his job over there.

He saw six soldiers lay in their blankets and a couple of the guards around the wagon dozed, then he signaled for Hacha to get ready and moved to the edge of the trees close to Uncle Ezra. Both tents in the clearing were dark.

Ben watched Hacha silently dispose of the sentry on this side, then he tossed an acorn to alert Uncle Ezra.

Ezra didn't turn, instead he touched Sergeant Gomez on the arm, then both men stood and moved next to the guards who were awake. At the same time, several *vaqueros* inched closer to the two soldiers who dozed near the wagons.

Ben looked up as the sun started to peek over the horizon, checked to make sure Hacha was ready, then gave the signal and stepped from cover with a pistol in each hand.

He moved swiftly across the clearing, but it seemed to Ben everything before him happened in slow motion. Out of the corner of his eye he saw Uncle Ezra and Sergeant Gomez disarm their guards, and the *vaqueros* swarm over two others.

Ben noted Paco and his men, along with Hacha and Paloma had the sleeping soldiers under their guns before the men could react and roll out of their blankets, then Ramon Padilla emerged from one of the tents with a musket in his hands.

Ben raised his pistol, but before he could fire, Joseph came around the corner to push Padilla's weapon down and caused it to discharge harmlessly into the ground.

Ben closed with Padilla before the Spaniard could reload and said, "Give it up, *Capitán.* You 'n your men are my prisoners."

Padilla surrendered his musket and blustered, "You can not do this to me. I am a representative of the King of Spain. I warn you. What you plan to do is against Spanish law."

Joseph said, "I explained to you, Ramon. Governor Galvez had applied for a special dispensation. We should have it before we reach the border."

Padilla sneered, "I do not believe you. Trade between the provinces of Texas and Louisiana is forbidden, and I do not intend for you and your 'yankee' friends to profit by stealing Spanish property."

Ben moved to the second tent, threw back the flap and went inside to make sure Pilar was all right, but was greeted instead by *Doña* Maria's formidable figure, and she definitely wasn't moving in slow motion.

She flailed away at his head and shoulders with thin cane and demanded, "Get out of here. This is the women's tent. You are not allowed."

He took the blows until he got a brief glimpse of Pilar, then sure that she was not injured, he beat a hasty retreat and almost ran over Uncle Ezra on the way out.

Ben paused to collect his wits, then with a wry grin on his face, he thought to himself. Last night he managed to capture over twenty men with only one harmless shot being fired, yet he'd just been put to rout by a single frail woman with a cane.

His uncle gave him a strange look, then said, "I got the soldier boys under guard and sent men for the ones ya left in the canyons. What're ya gonna do about the gal?"

Ben shook his head to clear it, then took a deep breath and said, "Damned if I know. Gettin' the cattle through is our main concern, we got to find a way to get it done. I'll worry about her when we get that figgered out. Bring Paco and Joseph to Padilla's tent for a powwow."

Ben paced back and forth around the table while he waited for the others. When they were all seated, he asked Joseph, "What tipped Padilla off?"

"Ramon is an ambitious man, anxious to be recognized by his superiors, but offered little chance of that here on the frontier. He was in *San Antonio de Bexár* last week, and I believe, even though he denies it, that he found out about the governor's letter. When he saw you at my *rancho*, he made the connection. Ramon knows it takes a long time to get approval from our government, so he decided to follow us. When he saw us gathering cattle, he took over the camp and planned to take us back to the capitol in chains before word came through. Ramon only waited for your return to supply additional proof of our guilt."

Ben waited for a moment, then said, "Always a chance we'd be discovered, but I thought it'd be after we started the drive. What we don't know is if Padilla told anybody else 'bout us."

Joseph said, "I do not believe Ramon would tell anyone."

"You really think he's that stupid?"

"I know he is that ambitious."

Hacha and Paloma entered the tent and Ben stood to introduce them, then studied his hands for a moment before he said, "We don't know if he was playin' a lone hand, but we gotta figger it that way. Hacha showed me how we can get the cattle t' the border. Question is, what to do with Padilla 'n his men. Can't just turn 'em loose. Even on foot, they'd be back on our trail in less'n a week."

"We can not kill them," Joseph said. "Those men only did as they were ordered."

"Don't want 'em dead. That's why I took the camp the way I did, but we've got to buy us some time. Only thing to do is take 'em with us." Then as if the matter was settled, Ben asked, "How many longhorns you got in the canyons?"

Joseph turned to Paco, who said, "Over a thousand, but we were unable to gather any since Ramon arrived."

"They'll have to do," Ben stated. "We got no more time."

Joseph asked, "How will we guard Padilla's men and drive the cattle at the same time? We don't have enough men."

Ben said, "Don't have any choice—at least for a while. Should be safe to turn 'em loose after we get through the mountains. Tell the men I want to move out of here soon as we get everybody fed."

Chapter Fifteen

BEN WALKED TO THE WOMEN'S tent, but this time, didn't barge in, instead he stopped outside to remove his cap and softly called out, "*Con permiso, Doña* Maria, I would speak with *la Señorita* Menchaca."

Voices that spoke in Spanish so fast Ben couldn't understand the words sounded from inside, then *Doña* Maria lifted back the flap, gave him a stony look, and said, "You may enter, but do not forget, I will be outside."

Ben closed the flap and turned to find Pilar standing next to him with a big smile on her face.

He got a lump in his throat at the sight of her, but asked gruffly, "What're you doin' here?"

Pilar moved so that her arm brushed against his, then looked up at him and said, "Are you not glad to see me, *mi amor?*"

Ben felt the heat rise in his collar at the question and stammered, "Sure, I'm glad to see you, or would be anywhere else, but this's no place for a woman."

Pilar stood on her tip-toes, put her arms around his neck and kissed Ben on the lips. With that done, she pulled back and said, "Well, I am glad to see you, and I did not mean to cause you concern, but I simply had no choice but to come."

Ben had a frown on his face when he asked, "But why?"

"Because daddy found out about us and he was furious."

"Found out 'what' about us?" Ben asked, his head starting to throb.

"Why, about us being in love, of course, and that we were going to be married. He threatened to whip me, and he has never done that, not one time in my whole life. Then he locked me in my room and said he would never permit our marriage, so I came here. Now we are free go away together."

Ben walked over and sat down to think. All he needed was more problems. Now Pilar's father'd be after 'em too, 'n even if he could spare the men for an escort, Ben wasn't at all sure he wanted to send her back.

Pilar put her hand on his shoulder and, with a tear in her eye, asked, "Did I do wrong?"

He stood up, took Pilar in his arms and stroked her back, then said, "No help for it now. Everything'll be all right. I'll take you 'n *Doña* Maria with us until we find a Spanish settlement where you'll be safe, 'n I'll come back for you after we finish the drive. Get ready to leave."

Pilar started to protest, then gave him a peck on the cheek and said demurely, "*Si, mi amor*, I will do as you wish."

Ben emerged from the tent to find the wagons packed and the *vaqueros* nearly finished with their meal.

He walked to the fire for a plate, then stopped near Uncle Ezra and said, "We're takin' the women with us. Keep an eye on 'em for me."

Ezra gave a big grin, then spit a stream of tobacco juice behind him and grumbled, "Sure 'nuf. 'Spect the next thing we'll be gettin' around here is a brass band. About all we need." Then he shuffled off to get his horse.

Joseph came up and said, "All is in readiness. Paco wants to talk to you before we leave. I understand Pilar is going with us."

Ben didn't want to talk about it any more, so he ignored the comment and walked away toward the rope corral.

Paco was talking to his men, so Ben went to saddle his silver stallion.

The *segundo* dismounted and said, "The cattle are split into two groups to make them easier to manage. My *vaqueros* have the longhorns from the first canyon already on the trail. We castrated six bulls to turn them into lead steers for each bunch, and the cows will follow the leaders, if we can make them move in the right direction. The problem is that the steers are not yet fully trained and it requires two men to handle them with each group. The longhorns will be spread out for miles, and the guards we must use on our prisoners and the ones assigned to protect the wagons, leave me without enough men to prevent the loss of cattle that stray from the herd."

Ben hated to lose any cows, but didn't know what more they could do, so he said, "Have to do the best we can."

"There may be another way," Paco said.

Ben jerked his head around and asked, "What'd you have in mind?"

"Padilla's men. Most of them are known to me."

Ben snapped his fingers and interrupted, "You think they might help us? Mite risky, but worth a try. Let's go talk to 'em."

They gathered the Spanish soldiers and Ben said, "You boys are gonna be with us for quite a spell. How you travel'll be up to you. We can put you on a rope tied to the wagon 'n let you walk, or you can give us your word that you won't try to get away and we'll give you a horse so you can help us with the cattle. You'll be workin' with our *vaqueros* and won't have any weapons or food. Also, we'll be in Comanche country, so if you decided to leave 'n we don't get you, the Indians will. What'd you say?"

Capitán Padilla drew himself up to his full five foot five and said, "This is inexcusable. We are soldiers of Spain, not nursemaids to cows. I demand to know how long you intend to keep us prisoner?"

"We'll release you soon's we're in the clear, 'n pay you *vaquero's* wages 'til we let you go. We'd rather trust you than guard you. Now, what's it gonna be?"

Padilla conferred with his men, then turned and said, "You have our word not to try to escape."

Ben smiled as he said, "Good. Paco, get our friends some horses, 'n let's get crackin'. Got us a ways to go."

Ben saw the wagons start out, then mounted and he and Hacha started down the trail. They passed the last of the longhorns coming out of the box canyon, and watched the riders in the rear and on the flanks chase back the strays and push the cattle out through the opening. The longhorns started to stretch out along the trail and soon the column narrowed to a width of only ten or twelve head.

They moved beside the lumbering beasts until they reached the front of the herd and Ben saw why extra riders were needed at the head of the column.

Three sets of steers were joined together at the neck by a wooden yoke similar to those Ben had seen used to help oxen pull in tandem back in the colonies. But these steers weren't being taught to pull, they were being trained to lead. Two thirty-foot ropes passed from the center of each yoke to the saddles of a *vaquero* on each side. The steers were in such close proximity that their long horns clashed against each other if they didn't walk straight ahead, and should one try to stray, the riders would pull the animal back in line.

Paco and Joseph caught up with them and Ben motioned to the steers and said, "Good idea. How'd you come up with it?"

Paco grinned and said, "One of the wagon drivers was a tiller of the soil and used this method to train farm animals. He suggested we give it a try and I think it will work. A few days in the yoke should make the steers into leaders."

Ben shook his head in agreement, then turned to Joseph and said, "It was awful easy to get Padilla to say he'd help us. Think we can trust him to keep his word?"

Joseph thought for a moment, then replied, "Under normal circumstances I would say yes, but in this case, I just don't know. What do you think, Paco?"

"I don't believe the soldiers will attempt anything unless ordered to do so by their *capitán*. I have assigned Sergeant Gomez to watch him and report anything suspicious." Paco looked back over his shoulder and continued, "My *vaqueros* do well, and with the addition of the men of Ramon, we will be able to push the cattle hard. They will tire by nightfall and be easier to handle. I think the cows will be broken to the trail by the time we get through the mountains. This would not be possible if we do not use his men."

"Looks like we got no choice," Ben said, "but I'll sleep a lot better when we get rid of 'em."

Paco clapped Ben on the shoulder and said, "Don't worry, *hermano*. We'll keep a close watch on him. Do you have a spot picked out for us to camp tonight?"

"Might take us 'til after dark to get there, but there's a stream surrounded by good grass about six miles ahead."

Paco nodded his head, gave a wave of his hand, then gigged his horse in the ribs and moved to the other side of the herd.

Ben sent Hacha to scout the trail, then reined his horse around to observe the riders work the cattle as he rode to the rear.

The *vaqueros* were well suited for their job. They rode loose in the saddle, but they and their horses worked as one. Their mounts many times would anticipate before its rider when a cow was about to break from the pack and move to keep the beast in line.

Padilla's men weren't as well mounted as the other riders, still the soldiers did manage to keep the cattle pretty well under control.

Ben stopped to let the last of the cows be driven by, then waited for the wranglers to bring the horses up. The herd was down to only two spare mounts for each rider—still, sixty to seventy animals were not easy for two men to handle. Next came the twenty bulls Joseph brought along so that the longhorns could procreate once the cattle were delivered to

Louisiana. To avoid trouble, they decided to keep the bulls separated from the cows until the end of the drive.

Ben arrived at the wagons to find them hidden in the cloud of dust created by the moving animals in front of them.

He tied his bandanna over his mouth, then eased his horse next to Uncle Ezra and said, "No reason for these wagons to be back here in all this."

Ezra nodded his head in agreement, so Ben dropped back by the supply wagons and told the drivers, "Pull out to the side and get out of the dust. Tomorrow we'll start you off first so you'll be at the front of the herd."

Ben reined along side Pilar's carriage and gave her driver the same orders. The curtains were dropped in the back, but as Ben spoke, he saw one pulled aside. Pilar appeared dusty and hot.

He pulled back beside the coach, removed his cap and asked, "You ladies all right? We'll have you out of this dust right soon now."

Pilar smiled and said, "We are just fine, thank you. Tell me, Mr. Cross, will we be able to bathe when we stop for the night?"

Ben, confused by her use of 'Mr. Cross,' managed to say, "I'll see what I can do, mam." The curtain fell back in place. Ben was left there to sit and stare after the departing carriage.

A gentle rain started to fall. He felt the drops brush against his face and looked up to the heavens, then slapped heels to his stallion's flanks to follow.

Ezra dropped back beside him and said, "Been meanin' t' talk to ya about that gal. What's goin' on between the two o' you?"

Ben scratched his chin and said, "Damned if I know, Uncle Ezra, but we got more immediate things to sort out right now."

Ezra sent a spray of brown juice streaking at a lizard that rested on a rock. He missed, then asked, "What about the Comanches on the other side of the mountain?"

Ben jerked his head around and asked, "How'd you know about the Indians? Hacha tell ya?"

Ezra nodded his head and Ben said, "Somethin' strange 'bout those braves. They're painted for war. No squaws with 'em, but it looked like they were settin' up a permanent camp. You know more about Indians 'n me. What'd make 'em do a thing like that?"

Ezra slowly stroked his beard, then said, "No way to tell for sure. Indians are notional folks. Do lots of things other people don't understand. Fifty braves is more'n usual for a hunting party, 'n them havin' paint on don't sound right. Maybe they'll be gone when we get there or could be they're an advance party 'n the rest of the village'll join 'em. I'll have me a look see when we get t' the mountains."

Ben had a grim look on his face when he said, "That camp's in spittin' distance of where we got to drive the cattle. Them Comanches ain't gone when we get there, we'll be in for a fight."

They looked at the sky and turned up their collars against the wet. The dust was settled now, replaced by clouds of steam that rose from the arid ground and the backs of the sweaty animals.

Ben said, "I figger the tail end of the herd back here's come three, maybe, four miles. The front ought be gettin' pretty close. Reckon I'll go up 'n guide 'em in."

He still didn't trust Padilla and kept an eye out for him as he rode to the front of the cattle. The soldiers he observed on the way seemed to be doing a good job minding the longhorns and he finally spotted the *capitán* with two of his men at the rear of the first bunch of cows. Sergeant Gomez was nearby, so Ben rode on.

The cattle smelled the water up ahead and Ben saw that the *vaqueros* now had a different problem. Instead of having to keep the beeves in line and moving down the trail, they now had to slow the leaders to prevent an all-out stampede.

The haze around the herd made it hard to see, but Ben finally picked out the figure of Hacha as he drew even with the lead steers.

Hacha reined in next to Ben and said, "All is well. The stream runs full and no sign of trouble."

He and Ben led the herd to the campsite, then splashed through the water to the far bank and turned to watch the cattle arrive.

Some of the cows splashed right into the stream and started to drink their fill, a few had to be roped and pulled from the stream before they foundered. The majority of the cattle waded in until their bellies were covered, then drank a little and moved on. A few only left the water when forced out by the buildup of longhorns behind them.

Ben watched the riders move the cattle in a wide circle when the animals emerged to graze, then force the lead cows back in toward the middle. Soon the beeves started to mill in on themselves and chomp on the lush grass. With thirst and hunger satisfied, the cattle lay down for the night. It was well after dark when the last of the cattle were bedded down and the *vaqueros* free to head for the cook wagon and something to eat.

Chapter Sixteen

BEN WAS UP BEFORE DAWN the next day and joined the night herders at the cook wagon. He stared over his coffee cup at the two men. The riders had turned in their night horses and would be lucky to get even an hour of sleep before they drew another and were back in the saddle to help move the herd.

Ben took his coffee and a plate of food down by the stream, then sat among the willows to wait for the rest of the camp to come to life.

He watched the wrangler bring in mounts gathered for the morning's work and drive them into a makeshift corral that consisted of ropes tied between trees and the wheels of the supply wagon.

The cook beat a metal rod against the triangle of iron mounted on his wagon to announce to the world that the morning meal was ready. The *vaqueros* came slowly out of their blankets, many of them with as little as four-hours rest. The men washed the sleep from their eyes, then put on their range clothes, poured a cup of scalding black coffee, and lined up for a plate loaded with beans and *tortillas*. The riders finished their meal, threw their bedrolls and blankets in the back of the supply wagon, then moved to the corral to rope the horse they chose to work with today.

Ben tossed away the last of his coffee, returned his utensils, then moved over to his roan and tightened the cinch. He'd decided to give the silver stallion some rest. He didn't work his horse as hard as the riders who tended the cattle, who sometimes changed mounts two or three times between daylight and dark. Still, Ben hated to work a horse two days in a row.

He looked over the top of his saddle and saw the wagons pull out. They would stay ahead of the longhorns and not have the dust from the herd to fight, but even more important, the early start made sure the cook would have time to prepare a hot meal and have it ready for the *vaqueros* when the cattle were bedded down for the night. Pilar's carriage trailed along with them.

Ben scratched his chin as he watched the figures retreat into the distance. He'd wanted to talk to Pilar last night, but the women were in bed by the time his work was done.

He wondered, for a moment, if she'd managed to get her bath, then turned to watch the riders saddle their ponies and top the horses off to work out the kinks.

The whole camp was moving now, so Ben climbed into the saddle and moved to the front of the herd.

The early morning clouds were burned off by the sun and the heat from above caused the cattle to stir and begin to lumber to their feet, then the *vaqueros* arrived and started to guide the longhorns onto the trail. The riders moved the lead steers out first while men in the rear and on the sides applied pressure to get the beeves spread out.

Both groups of cattle were lined out and drifted east by mid-morning. Paco and his men pushed the longhorns hard in the hope this would gentle the cattle and make them more manageable.

Ben scouted ahead where he found the trail clearly marked and easy to follow, so he turned back and reined in beside the lead riders.

Joseph greeted him and said, "It goes well. At this pace, we will soon reach the mountains."

"Been thinkin' on that," Ben replied. "We need to make some plans. I'll talk to Uncle Ezra and Hacha. Tell Paco we'll meet at your tent after camp settles down tonight."

Joseph looked at Ben with troubled eyes, then said, "I will speak to Paco."

Ben rode silently for a moment, then turned and said, "'Nother thing you need to know. About Hacha 'n Paloma."

"The Indians who helped us? Is there a problem?"

"Could be. Hacha is full-blood Yaqui. Paloma is Apache. Their tribes are enemies, so they ran away when they were kids. Wound up at a Spanish mission named *Ysleta* somewhere to the south. The *Padre* there took 'em in, fed 'em 'n taught 'em to speak Spanish and English, even gave 'em Spanish names."

"Yes, I wondered about that. His name stands for axe in your language and hers means dove, but I do not understand what the problem is."

Ben pulled his horse up and said, "Three soldiers got drunk 'n tried to rape Paloma. Hacha killed the men 'fore they left the mission."

Joseph stopped also, wrinkled his brow in thought, then said, "I remember now. The incident happened several years ago. They have nothing to fear from the authorities. The *Padre* found out the truth of the matter and cleared their names."

Ben, obviously relieved, smiled and said, "They're good people. I'll tell 'em the news," then he slapped the roan in the ribs and rode to the east.

There was no place on the trail they could hide from the heat of the afternoon sun, and the riders were forced to change horses often, but the weather seemed to make the longhorns more docile and easier to drive.

The herd caught up with the wagons before nightfall because the cattle smelled water by mid-afternoon and the *vaqueros* had no trouble moving the cows ahead to the small lake where they planned to camp.

Ben raised the flap to enter Joseph's tent after supper to find the others already seated at the table inside.

He sat down and said, "Way things're goin', we'll be to the foothills in two . . . three days. Well in range of the bucks in the canyon. If the Indians are there or even in the mountains, we got to know about it. I want Uncle Ezra to check out the Comanche camp. Hacha can guide him to it."

Ben turned to his uncle and said, "If them bucks are still in the canyon, see if you think there's a way around them. We can't take the cattle to the north, that's back into the middle of Indian country. I'm gonna scout south of here to see if there's another way to go if the Comanches still block our way."

He looked at Joseph and said, "Take us a couple a days. Think you 'n Paco can handle things here 'til we get back?"

"We will manage until you return." Joseph said with a nod of his head.

Paco spoke up, "You should not do this thing alone, *hermano*. I will go with you, or at least take Sergeant Gomez."

Ben stood up, put his hand on the *segundo's* shoulder and said, "You're needed here, my friend, 'n the sergeant must guard Padillo. I'll be all right."

There were no more comments, so he said, "That's it then. We'll lay in some fresh meat for the cook 'fore we go and start out at first light."

BEN TOPPED THE ridge a few miles from where he planned to meet the herd and looked up in the clear, moonlit sky to check the position of the big dipper in relation to the north star and saw the time was a little after midnight.

Ben was tired to the bone and the quiver he felt between his legs told him his mount was in much the same shape. They'd been on the move since the morning they left the herd, most of two days, with only a few hours rest in between. He slumped forward to pat the silver stallion on the neck and said, "Won't be long now, boy. Give you a rubdown 'n turn you out to pasture, soon's we get t' camp."

Ben had been taken by the wild, untamed beauty of the country as he moved to the south, but ran into heavy brush and dense mesquite thickets before he'd ridden half a day. He circled to the east until the brush forced him into a low marshy area covered with stagnant water. The swamp stretched for miles, so far that Ben couldn't see to the other side. He rode well into the night and tested the mushy land all the way to where it butted up against cliffs to the south, but never found a place firm enough for them to drive the cattle.

Ben finally decided there was no way through and caught a couple hours sleep, then started back. He rode throughout the day, and since he had a clear, cloudless sky, decided to ride into the night. Now that he knew they no longer had the option of to drive the cattle south around the mountains, he was eager to get back so he could find out what Uncle Ezra had discovered.

He moved through the trees for another hour, then paused when the outline of bunched horses appeared in front of him. Ben knew he was close because the remuda would be less than half a mile from camp.

Something about the scene bothered Ben, but he couldn't put his finger on what it was. Then he knew. No rider was with the horse herd.

Ben quickly dismounted and crept forward on foot. He moved to the edge of the trees and his eyes swept the clearing, but found nothing out of the ordinary until he spotted a dark object on the ground near some low hanging branches. Ben lay his rifle down and checked to make sure his pistol was primed, then crept around the edge of the trees.

He moved close enough to see the form on the ground was that of a man and when he spotted no movement around him, Ben stepped into the clearing and stopped beside the still figure.

He knelt to turn the fallen man over, then started to twist toward a sound behind him and the world around him exploded in a flash of thunder and lightning enveloped his mind and shut down his brain.

* * *

BEN STRUGGLED TO rise from the depths of unconsciousness, his first sensation one of intense pain from the back and right side of his head. He struggled to clear the cobwebs and almost panicked when he realized he didn't have any idea where he was.

Ben slowly opened his eyes, and when they came into focus, he saw it was daylight and he was nestled against something soft. He glanced around and saw he lay on his left side in the back of the supply wagon, then looked up to gaze into the tear-streaked face of Pilar. Her eyes showed concern and were red and puffy.

He opened his mouth to say something, but no words came out. Next, he struggled to turn and sit up, but was prevented from doing so by strong hands that held him down, and the sudden shock of pain that coursed through his body and caused him to fall back.

Pilar gave a little sob at the sign of his movement, stroked his face and said, with tears in her voice, "Do not move, *mi amor*. You will break open your wound."

Uncle Ezra tilted Ben's head to give him a drink of water, then growled in a voice choked with emotion, "Lay back, boy. Little rest, 'n you'll be fine as can be."

The water seemed to clear his throat a little, but Ben decided he needed something stronger to shock his senses, so he croaked, "Whiskey."

Uncle Ezra's search of the wagon produced a jug and he poured first a little, then a generous slug of the fiery liquid into his nephew's mouth. The liquor burned all the way down and brought tears to Ben's eyes, then almost came back up when it hit his stomach, but at the same time cleared the haze from his mind.

He coughed once, gulped to hold everything down, then looked up at his uncle and asked, "What happened?"

"It was Padilla 'n some of his men. They bashed Gomez

over the head, then knifed one of the wranglers. You come on 'em when they was after the horses, 'n they shot ya. Hacha 'n me are gettin' ready to go after 'em."

Ben lifted his eyes and asked, "Padilla got away?"

Ezra nodded. "Him 'n four of his men. We was to late t' stop 'em. They drove the horse herd off, 'n headed north, but don't worry, we'll get 'em back."

Ben struggled to rise. His skull still hurt like crazy, but the strength was slowly returning to his body and finally, with Pilar and Ezra's help, he was able to sit up.

His hands went to his head and he gingerly felt of the bandages there, then said, "No, wait. First of all, how bad am I hurt?"

Ezra gave a grim smile and said, "Wal, you got lucky there, old hoss, or maybe it's just your hard head. You were shot from behind at point blank range, so close the blast burned all the hide plum off your coon skin cap 'n some o' your hair along with it, but the slug must a hit at an angle. The ball went into the back o' your head, hit your skull, then furrowed 'round under the skin 'n come out over your right ear. Figger you're due to have a hell of a headache, but after some rest, you'll be on your feet in no time."

Pilar interrupted, "Yes, he needs his rest. You can talk to him tomorrow."

Ben smiled at Pilar and patted her hand as if to say, just a little while longer, then took the jug from his uncle and after a long drink, he turned to Joseph and asked, "Any idea where Padilla's headin'?"

"There is only one place he could be going. *El Fuerte del Cibolo*, an outpost to the north of here that has a garrison of twenty soldiers."

"How far away?"

"A two or three day ride."

Ben turned back to Ezra and said, "Forget Padilla. Send Hacha after the horses. They're more important 'n he is.

We'll just have to get the cattle 'cross the border 'fore the soldiers catch up with us."

"Now, what'd you find in the mountains?"

Ezra scratched his chin and said, "Ain't gonna be easy. Comanches're still camped in the valley. More 'n when you were there, maybe sixty, seventy strong 'n more comin' in. No Indian sign this side of the mountains, but we got no chance of takin' the cattle through without the Comanches knowin'."

Ben's head and shoulders sagged, then Pilar gently massaged his neck and he looked up said, "Didn't find a place to take the cattle 'round to the south. We got to take 'em through the mountains. There's got to be a way."

Ezra stared at his nephew for a moment, then patted his arm and said, "You're 'bout done in, boy. Get some rest. We'll study on it tomorrow."

Ben felt himself fall back. He closed his eyes, his head nestled against the softness of Pilar's lap. The last thing he heard before consciousness slipped from his mind was her voice saying, "Yes, rest now, my sweet."

Chapter Seventeen

BEN DIDN'T OPEN HIS EYES the next morning until he was jolted back to consciousness when the front wheels of the wagon bounced through a rut in the trail. He pushed his back against the side boards and closed his eyes to let his head clear.

Ben sensed movement and turned to find Pilar a few feet from him, a look of concern on her face.

She swabbed him with a damp rag and said, "Lay back. It is too soon for you to move about. Do you wish to eat?"

He gave her a weak smile, then said, "'Spect you're right 'bout movin'. Some grub 'n somethin' to drink might help."

"I knew you would be hungry. I have a deer steak and beans for you. I will get your coffee."

Ben watched Pilar climb nimbly over the tailgate of the slow moving wagon, then drop off onto the trail and wondered if he heard her right about the coffee. She returned minutes later, climbed back in and handed him the plate of food along with a cup of black liquid that was hot to the touch when he gripped it.

He stared at her in wonderment and asked, "Where'd you get hot coffee on the trail?"

She shrugged her shoulders and said, matter of factly, "I have cook put some in the fire pot under his wagon for you."

Ben took a sip, then choked the tears from his eyes and said, "That's some strong coffee."

Pilar's lips curled up in a smile, then she said, "It is half rum, to help you heal."

He wolfed down the steak and beans, then had another cup of the potent mixture while Pilar tended his wound and put on a new bandage.

Ben could feel the strength return to his abused body. The day and night of rest had allowed his tired muscles to recover from his long scout and the effects of the gunshot. The wound would cause him problems for a while, but he decided his skull wasn't cracked, so he'd recover soon enough.

Ben used the stays of the wagon cover to pull himself to his feet and after a short spell of dizziness, found he could stand on his own.

Pilar moved to help support him, but he said, "It's all right. I can manage."

She refused to move, instead she stamped her foot and fussed at him, "You most certainly are not all right. You are weak as a kitten and I demand that you sit back down. I will not allow you to leave this wagon until you are well."

Ben stared down at her, so shocked by the fury of her outburst that he quickly took a seat.

He recovered somewhat, then said, "I got to talk to Uncle Ezra. We need to figger out what we're gonna do."

Pilar crossed her arms in front of her chest, "Your uncle can come to the wagon later, then you can talk."

Ben suddenly realized he might be pushing it a little bit, so he leaned back against the side and closed his eyes for just a minute.

The next thing he knew was when Uncle Ezra shook him and said, "Time t' wake up, boy. It's past noon."

Ben sat up and wiped the sleep from his eyes, then stretched his muscles and noticed he felt better. . . stronger.

He yawned, then looked across and said, "Sorry 'bout sleepin' so long. What's going on out there?"

Ezra gave a grim smile and said, "Don't worry 'bout

that. You needed the rest. Fact is, I'm on orders from the little lady here, not to tire you out."

Ben glanced at Pilar and saw the determined look on her face, then turned back to Uncle Ezra and asked, "Hear anythin' from Hacha?"

Ezra nodded his head. "Got back 'bout an hour ago, but he only got half o' the remuda and didn't see anythin' o' Padilla or his men."

"Damn, that's gonna be a problem. If our riders don't have enough mounts to change off during the day, the horses won't last to the end of the drive."

Pilar said, "You can get more ponies in *Natchitoches*."

"That's all the way to the border. We'd never make it that far with the mounts we have."

"Might not make no difference," Ezra said, "'Less we can figger out a way t' get 'round the Comanches."

Ben just sat there, his mind in a whirl, then he snapped his fingers and said, "I got an idea. Might just solve all our problems."

Ezra stared at his nephew like Ben had lost his mind, then said, "Wal, I'd like to hear that, I surely would. Could be, you been takin' too many blows to the head, but I'm a listenin'."

"Get me a piece of paper 'n somethin' to draw with," Ben said, excitement in his voice.

Pilar got the items Ben requested and he drew a crude map, then showed it to Ezra and asked, "This the way you remember the Indian camp bein' laid out?"

Ezra studied the paper for a moment, then said, "Yeah, 'bout like that. The Comanches was right here at the north entrance t' the canyon, with trees like you show on one side 'n the face of a cliff on the other."

Ben sat back, then asked, "Where was the pony herd located?"

"The horses were in the trees, same place they was when you 'n Hacha scouted 'em, but you ain't plannin' t' steal the

Indian ponies, are ya? Can't be done without them knowin'. Sixty, seventy braves was in that camp when I's there, could be a hundred by now. That's better'n two t' one 'gainst us. Be plain suicide to try."

"What if I can show you a way to change the odds? Put 'em better'n ten to one in our favor?"

Ezra stared at his nephew in disbelief, then asked, "You got a secret army 'round here, you ain't told us 'bout?"

Ben smiled and said, "Yep, got me over a thousand of the meanest critters God ever put on four legs."

Ezra slapped his hand against his leg and said with a smile on his face, "The cattle. You want to run 'em through the Indian camp. Tell me how you want t' do it. Might work, by golly, just might work."

Ben's look became somber when he said, "There's maybe one chance in a hundred we can get the cattle through without the Comanches attacking the herd, 'n if we do, that don't mean they won't find out 'n come after us. Even if we can slip by the Indians, we don't have the horses to finish the drive, so I don't see we got any choice but to make it work.

"We'll stampede the cattle through the camp at midnight, most of the braves'll be settled down by then. Hacha says there's fresh water five or six miles after we get out of the canyon, so to give the cows more reason to run, we won't give 'em any water the night before 'n none the next day. By the time we're ready to turn 'em loose, the longhorns'll run over anything between them 'n water—least they better."

Ezra was showing a little more enthusiasm now. He asked, "What about the Indian ponies?"

"That's our job. You, me, 'n Hacha. We'll go in early to get in position. When the cattle hit the camp, we'll drive off the whole pony herd. The Comanches can't follow us without horses 'n we'll have enough mounts to finish the drive. Paco and Joseph can start the stampede, then we'll all meet at the water when the longhorns stop to drink."

Ezra sat back for a moment, then stood up and said, "Any other way t' go, I'd be against it. Too risky, but like you say, we got no choice. I'll fill the others in on our plans."

Ben lay his head back after his uncle left, then a thought hit him and he turned to Pilar and asked, "How is it *Doña* Maria lets you stay with me?"

Pilar smiled and gave a laugh that had a musical lilt to it, then said, "She had no choice in the matter, but I will say she did not object too strongly. I think she likes you."

Ben snorted, "She's got a strange way a showing it."

Pilar placed her hand on his arm and said, "You must understand. She is of the old ways, she and my father both. They are of the Spanish aristocracy, and do not want to believe this is a new country with new ways. I know they love me and believe they know what is best for me, but only I can make that decision, and I have. I have told them both that I love you, but only Maria has accepted it. She will help us when the time comes, I know she will . . . if you feel the same about me?"

Ben looked at her. He wished she wasn't even here because of the danger, but when he thought about how he felt when she was near, he was glad she was.

He took Pilar in his arms and said, "All I know is when you're not around me, the sun is not as bright. The air not so clear. The flowers don't smell as sweet, and the days are much too long. I'm not too good with words, but that's the way I feel. I reckon that's love."

Pilar pushed back so she could look into his eyes and said, "Why, Ben Cross, that is quite the most romantic speech I have ever heard. It is much more important to feel love than to talk about it."

She gave him a slow lingering kiss, then lightly stroked his cheek and said, "Rest now, *mi amor*, you must regain your strength."

* * *

BEN SAT IN the saddle of his silver stallion two nights later, his wounds forgotten. The headaches were no longer a problem and he sported only a small bandage under the borrowed *sombrero* he wore.

He looked up at the sky and smiled. Conditions were ideal for the attack. The weather was overcast, with a hint of rain in the air and the moon completely hidden behind a thick layer of dense churning clouds.

Ben watched the riders mill the cattle in a circle. They were in position several miles from the Indian camp, ready to start the stampede when he and the others were in place at the pony herd. The longhorns were thirsty and restless from lack of water and bleated and mooed to show their displeasure. The strong north wind kept the noise from reaching the Indian camp and at the same time carried the scent of water to the cattle.

Ben moved over to check on Pilar and *Doña* Maria. They were in the supply wagon since it had thick wooden sides and was more sturdy than their carriage. Padilla's soldiers who remained had no choice but to help in the fight, so he armed the men and placed six of them in each wagon and two more in the carriage.

Ben gave two of his pistols, along with powder and shot to Pilar and said, "Keep down and don't use these unless an Indian gets on the wagon. If that happens, pull this hammer all the way back 'n aim the weapon just like you'd point your finger, then squeeze the trigger."

She listened intently, then said, "Do not worry about me. I have hunted before. It is you who must be careful."

He leaned down to kiss her and said, "See you on the other side," then rode to where Joseph waited.

Ben stopped his horse and said, "We'll be in position in two hours. Remember to keep the wagons close to the back of the herd. We don't want to give the Indians a chance to recover 'fore the wagons roll through."

Joseph's face was grim as he said, "It will be done. Go with God, my friend."

Ezra rode up and said, "Hacha's gone ahead to check on the guards. He'll meet us this side of the trees."

Ben and Ezra pushed hard and less than an hour later the figure of Hacha emerged from the gloom in front of them.

The Yaqui stopped beside them and whispered, "Camp is asleep. Two braves guard horses. One this side, other is on the far edge of trees."

Ben leaned over and asked, "Can we get close to 'em?"

"There is cover to within bow range."

"All right, then. We kill the guards soon as we can work our way close enough. Hacha, you take the one on the far side, then signal me 'n I'll get the one over here. Uncle Ezra, get between us 'n the camp to stop anyone headed this way."

They tied their horses to a tree and moved slowly forward.

Ben crawled through the bushes, then rose to his feet behind a big oak tree near the pony herd. His eyes searched the area until he spotted the guard near a small fire some fifty feet away. Ben moved to the side so he had a clear shot, then nocked an arrow in case the brave looked his way.

Ben was in position for only a few minutes when the hoot of an owl sounded three times in quick succession from the other side of the bunched horses.

He drew the bow back until his left arm was fully extended, took a deep breath, then released the string from the fingers of his right hand to launch the arrow on its way. The shaft buried itself with a loud thud in the chest of the Comanche. No sound came from the man's open mouth, instead, a sudden gush of blood flowed over the Indian's hands when they clutched at the feathered shaft, then fell away as the brave crumpled to the ground.

Ben looked toward the camp and saw no sign of move-ment, no indication they'd been discovered, then turned back as Hacha appeared beside him.

Ezra brought up the horses and said, "Won't be long now," then they mounted to wait for Joseph and the others.

Hacha turned toward the sound first, then Ben and Ezra. A low rumbling noise came from the valley to their right, then near a thousand thirst-crazed cattle burst over a ridge barely a hundred yards away. The fast moving longhorns sent a cloud of dust toward the heavens. Out of the dust came a sound that echoed across the land like thunder and caused the ground to tremble around them.

Ezra and Hacha yelled and waved blankets over their heads to stampede the pony herd. Ben stayed with them until the horses were out of the valley, then he doubled back to check on what happened in the village.

He moved back into the edge of the trees to observe the scene below him and found the camp a shambles. The Comanches had been caught off guard, many of them still in their beds, when the longhorns overran the village. Some braves died on the horns of the hard charging cattle, others were trampled into dust by the pounding hooves of the longhorns. A few bucks were cut down by shots from the fast riding *vaqueros* and the accurate fire from soldiers in the wagons.

Ben saw several Comanches reach the face of the cliff and scramble among the rocks to avoid the slaughter, while other braves managed to reach ponies tied next to their tepees and get out ahead of the charge.

He saw an Indian grab onto the back of the supply wagon and pull himself above the tailgate, then fall back, his face a mass of blood. Another brave tried to grab the horses that pulled the cook wagon, but missed his grip and met his death under the spinning wheels.

Ben shot a Comanche before the brave made the cover of the trees and recharged his rifle, but before he could fire again, the last of the cattle and wagons raced out of the canyon into the open expanse of the prairie. The encounter had lasted less than ten minutes, but the carnage and devastation of the camp was complete.

Ben checked, but didn't see any of their men down in the village, so he wheeled his stallion and caught up with the last wagon, then had the driver pull up at the mouth of the canyon.

He dismounted and ordered the soldiers out of the wagon into the rocks where they could cut off pursuit from the village.

Ben shot the first Comanche out of the canyon, then watched the other braves turn back after they lost four of their number in the first volley from the soldiers.

Ben figured the Indians wouldn't be back, so he sent the wagon on ahead, but he trailed behind, just in case.

Chapter Eighteen

BEN PASSED THE BODIES OF forty or fifty longhorns and several horses on the plains before he caught up with the herd. He reached the stream by mid-morning and found that the cattle had run themselves out and were either in the water or rested on the far bank.

The wagons were pulled off to one side, near the cook fire and upwind from the longhorns. The aroma of coffee drew Ben in that direction.

He dismounted and accepted a cup of the hot liquid from Pilar, then asked, "You all right?"

Pilar came into his arms and said, "I am not hurt, but the soldier beside me in the wagon was killed."

Ben gave her a hug, then she stepped back and said, "Sit down over here. You have opened the wounds on your head."

Pilar replaced his bandages, then Ben turned to Joseph and said, "Didn't see none of our riders go down. We lose anybody else?"

"We were fortunate. The soldier in the freight wagon was the only casualty. A number of the men have slight wounds, but none are serious."

Ben took a long drink of coffee and said, "Better double the guard tonight. Not enough Comanches left back there to attack us, but they might try to sneak in here 'n get some of their ponies back."

Ezra walked up from the edge of the water with a big grin on his face and clapped Ben on the back when he said, "We done it, boy. Slickest bit o' horse stealin' I ever did see. Them Comanches never knew what hit 'em. Don't have to worry about them no more."

Ben looked to see his uncle wasn't hurt, then said dryly, "Not that bunch anyhow. Problem is, there's lots more Indians 'tween us 'n where we got to go. How many ponies in that bunch we run off?"

"Got here with near two hundred o' them little mustangs. We got no more remount problems. Riders'll have t' change horses more, but we got enough for 'em to do that now."

Pilar returned Ben's pistols and he noticed one had been fired, but was properly recharged. He looked at her quizzically.

She gave a shrug of her shoulders and said, "An Indian tried to climb in the wagon."

Ben grinned as he remembered seeing the Indian fall and said, "Saw him go down."

Paco rode up and dismounted, then walked over to Ben and said, "Your plan was a good one, *hermano*. Many Comanches met their maker last night, and the ones left should cause us no trouble without horses."

Ben thought for a moment, then said, "Could be you're right, but those Indians came from somewhere. If their village ain't too far away, the braves that are left might get some help 'n come after us. Uncle Ezra 'n me'll go back 'n scout the camp after we get some food."

Paco nodded his head and said, "I think that is wise. We will allow the wounded to rest for today and tonight to recover before we push on."

Ben finished eating, then told Paco, "Hacha'll show you the way back to the trail if we're not back 'fore you pull out. We'll catch up."

*　*　*

THE SUN WAS low in the western sky by the time Ben and Ezra topped the rim of the cliff that overlooked the canyon. They'd come up the eastern slope of the mountain and left their horses tied half way up, then climbed the rest of the way on foot, the last fifty yards on their bellies. They moved into rocks high above the Comanche camp and studied the scene below.

Ben counted half a dozen braves moving around in the remains of the Indian village, all of whom had an injury of some kind, then Uncle Ezra pointed out ten or so more that lay on blankets in the shade on the far side.

Ben used his glasses to penetrate the shadows and spotted several horses picketed under cover of the trees, but he failed to find any guards posted anywhere.

Ezra nudged Ben and pointed toward the mouth of the canyon where three mounted Comanches rode out of sight over a small rise in the prairie. The braves were riding north.

Ben motioned Uncle Ezra back from the edge and said, "Stay here 'til dark 'n see what goes on in camp. I'll follow those bucks 'n see where they're headed. I'm not back by mornin', you catch up with the herd."

Ben went back down the hill to the horses. He tightened the cinch on his saddle, then mounted the silver stallion and circled to the north.

Ben picked up the Indian's trail on the prairie after he was out of sight of the canyon, then looked up at the sky and figured there was maybe two hours of daylight left. The braves were more 'n an hour ahead of him, so he urged his horse into a gallop to try and close the distance between them.

Ben felt the big stallion's hooves eat up the miles, but the cloak of darkness settled around him before he caught sight of the riders ahead.

He didn't know if the braves would stop for the night or not, but Ben didn't want to stumble on them in the dark, so he pulled up in some cottonwoods at the edge of a river.

Ben let his horse drink, took some water himself, then climbed a tree to see if he could spot a campfire on the trail ahead. He waited for two hours, then decided the Indians hadn't stopped, or at least not close enough for him to see their fire.

He dropped to the ground and a slight noise in the bushes alerted him. Ben started to turn, then an arrow slammed into the tree where his head rested moments before. He drew his pistols as he dove swiftly to the ground and landed on his stomach with his arms extended in front of him.

His weapons cocked, he searched in the darkness for a target. Ben glanced up at the tree, and the angle of the shaft that still quivered there showed him the shot came from behind him. He wondered if the braves he followed had spotted him and doubled back, if this was a different bunch. It crossed his mind that if he was forced to shoot and this wasn't the same Indians he trailed, the Comanches ahead of him could come back and get him in a cross fire.

Ben wondered why no more arrows followed the first, and looked longingly at the bow tied to his horse. He started to inch his way in that direction but before he could reach the stallion, Ben was confronted with wildly yelling Indians that rushed at him out of the darkness. He spotted at least four and his reactions were instinctive. He quickly rose to meet the charge and, no longer able to worry about the noise, pulled the trigger of his right hand pistol.

Fire and smoke exploded from the muzzle of his weapon and lit up the night. He saw the lead ball strike an Indian in the chest, then fired his left hand pistol into the stomach of a Comanche and the man went to his knees with his hands clutched at his middle.

Ben dodged to the side and threw his empty gun at a brave on the right. Blood spurted from warrior's face when the heavy weapon struck him full across the nose, and the Comanche dropped like a stone.

He dodged to his left and ducked inside the downward swipe of the last Comanche's tomahawk, but dropped his other pistol in doing so.

Ben hammered his fist into the brave's throat. The Indian staggered back from the force of the blow, then regained his balance and surged forward with his axe raised above his head.

Ben pulled a knife from his belt, then grabbed the charging Indian's arm with his left hand and thrust forward with his right. He felt the point of his blade meet resistance against the corded muscles of the Comanche's stomach, then sink in until the hilt rested against flesh. Ben jerked his fist upward and the razor sharp edge of his knife sliced the Indian open from belly to rib cage. The blade hung against a bone and was pulled from Ben's hand when the brave fell into his own blood and intestines on the sand.

A powerful arm gripped him from behind and Ben thought at first it was the warrior he hit in the face with his gun, but when he twisted in that direction to try and break the hold, that brave was still on the ground.

Ben struggled to remove the arm from around his neck, but the Comanche's grip was too strong, so he used his legs to push his body back into the chest of the warrior. The momentum carried both men over the river bank and down into the swirling brown water.

The shock of the fall loosened the Indians throttle hold, and Ben struggled to get his eyes above water to locate the warrior. He got his hands around the brave's neck to force the man's head under the river, but Ben's strength was fading and the Comanche broke away.

He dove after the Indian and grappled with him, then a shot sounded and Ben was thrown to one side when the body of a dead Comanche landed in the river.

Ben shook the water from his eyes, then glanced toward the river bank and saw Ezra lower a smoking gun from his shoulder, then his uncle shouted, "Catch," and launched a knife in Ben's direction.

The warrior saw the blade coming too, but Ben went high out of the water so his fingers closed around the handle of the weapon first. His body came down on top of the brave and forced them both under the river. The arm with the knife rose high above the water, slashed down, then rose and fell again.

The river around Ben was red with blood when he released the Indians body and let it float down stream.

He made his way to the edge of the river and leaned against the bank, then looked up and said, "'Preciate the use of the knife. How'd you happen to be here, anyway?"

Ezra extended his hand to help Ben up to dry land and said, "Buck come in off the prairie couple hours after you left. This bunch headed out in your direction 'n I figgered I better trail along in case they was after you."

"Damn near got me too. Had me pinned down. Barely missed with an arrow, but they never fired again."

Ben sat with his back against a tree for a moment to rest, then got to his feet when his uncle returned with the Indian ponies in tow.

Ezra handed Ben an Indian bow and said, "Only found one, 'n it's busted. Reckon that's why they never shot at you but once. Must of lost the rest of their weapons in the stampede."

Ben nodded his head, then asked, "Anythin' happen at the Comanches' camp?"

"Not much. They was tendin' to their wounded 'n buildin' racks to put their dead on."

Ben gave his uncle a strange look and Ezra said, "Paco told me about it. Seems the Comanches honor their dead, but don't believe in puttin' 'em in the ground. Something about the dead Indian's spirit being trapped 'n not able to get to the happy huntin' ground.

"Anyway, the Comanches build a bed on some sticks, out a the reach of varmints, 'n put the bodies on it. Usually in some secret place, but with as many dead as they got back there, I figger the Indians decided to put 'em to rest where they was."

Ben scratched his chin and said, "Seems mighty strange to me, but I guess folks can do what ever they like."

He picked up the pistol he'd thrown and placed it in his belt after he checked and recharged the weapon, then walked over to the dead Indians and said, "Help me throw these other bucks 'n the river, then we'll move up stream 'n get some rest."

They pulled into a secluded gully two hours later and built a small fire.

Ezra made coffee, then handed Ben a cup and asked, "What 'bout them braves you was tailin'? Any idea where they're headin'?"

"Never caught up with 'em, but I was close enough to see their fire if they stopped for the night, so they must of rode on. I figger the Indians are headin' for their village to get help. No way to tell if they'll come after us, but the Comanches ain't gonna be too happy about us killin' those braves back in the canyon, so we better plan on 'em chasin' us down. Question is, when."

Ezra looked up between the overhanging limbs and said, "Gonna rain. Maybe it'll wash out our tracks."

Ben snorted. He knew better and Uncle Ezra did too. He figured his uncle didn't really expect an answer, so Ben didn't give him one. Instead, he poured the last of his coffee in the fire and unrolled his blankets.

He lay there listening to the pleasant cooing of the doves, and the gentle rustle of the leaves in the breeze. Ben thought about how peaceful it was here and as he tried to fall asleep, he wondered what tomorrow would bring.

Chapter Nineteen

BEN DIDN'T GET MUCH REST. He watched thunder and lightning dance across the sky to the north for several hours then, shortly after midnight, the heavens opened up to a drenching rain that moved in on them and invaded their shelter.

Ben rolled out of his soaked blankets and saw that the weather upstream had swelled the river from its banks and turned the gentle rolling stream into a raging torrent. He and Ezra scrambled to collect their gear, but were still forced to lead the Indian ponies through water that swirled up past the belly of the horses in order to reach higher ground.

They stopped in the edge of a huge oak tree grove to wait for the lighting to pass, then hunched their shoulders and rode out onto the prairie. They were well out in the open when the wind suddenly started to whip the rain sideways with such velocity that the drops stung like the bite of a hornet when the tiny pellets struck exposed skin.

Ben nudged his stallion into a gallop and led the way to an overhang in a deep buffalo waddie for shelter. He and Ezra dismounted and calmed the horses, then sat against the wall to wait until the wind slacked off.

Ezra leaned next to Ben and asked, "You gonna turn them soldier boys loose now that the cattle are out of the mountains?"

"Told 'em I would."

"Extra guns'd come in handy, them Comanches catch up to us, Ezra mused. "Could be, with their captain gone, they might want t' stay."

Ben thought for a moment, then shrugged his shoulders and said, "Their choice. Soldiers don't want to go, we sure won't run 'em off. Storm's died down. Let's get back to the herd."

The fresh smell of the land being washed clean lingered after the rain stopped, then they closed on the trail the herd traveled and the odor of death assailed their nostrils.

They stopped on a small rise and Ben looked up at the vultures that circled lazily against the background of the dark clouds, then at the birds already on the ground that pecked at the scattered corpses of the longhorns lost in the stampede. He watched wolves, some of 'em big as a year-old calf, fight each other for their share of the carrion, while their little brothers, the coyote, slunk around the edge of the dead cattle and looked for a chance to steal any tiny scrap of meat.

Ezra spurted a stream of tobacco juice at nothing in particular, then said, "Good book says God had a reason for ever' livin' creature he put on this here earth, but when it comes to coyotes, I'll be damned if I can figger out what his idea was."

Ben didn't answer, just grinned and nudged his horse in the ribs to ride around the carnage.

They caught up with the men riding drag on the cattle at mid-day, then went to the remuda and turned over the Indian ponies to the wrangler. They changed horses and two hours later reached the front of the herd and the wagons.

Joseph lifted his hand in greeting, then rode up to Ben and said with a smile, "We were concerned for your safety, my friend. What have you learned?"

"The Comanches back there were pretty well cut up. Not more 'n a handful of bucks still able to fight. Problem is, three braves rode off to the north late yesterday. I tried to follow 'em, but didn't catch up, so we don't know for sure where they were goin'."

Uncle Ezra said gruffly, "Got a good idea, though."

Joseph looked first at Ezra, then back to Ben and asked, "You believe the Comanches went back to their village and will come after us?"

"That'd be my guess. Course, if we can move the longhorns along fast enough, might not make no difference. Depends on how far those bucks have to go to get help, so we'll have to keep an eye out, just in case. How'd the cattle take it when the storm came through?"

Joseph elevated his eyebrows and said, "It was a close thing. I think we were lucky the herd was still tired from the other night. The cows were frightened by the thunder and lightning. They tried to run, but the *vaqueros* were ready and managed to stop the longhorns from bolting. I doubt if the night guards alone would have been able to control the cattle."

Paco rode up and said, "*Hola! hermano.* It goes well, no? Hacha tells me the country from here to the border is lush and easy to travel through. Tonight we camp on the banks of The *Rio* Trinity and three days later, we reach the Neches. Two days more and we cross the *Rio* Sabine and have a clear path to Louisiana."

Ben smiled and said, "Maybe the worst part's behind us."

He turned to Joseph and asked, "How go's it with Padilla's men? Have you told them they could leave yet?"

"I offered them their freedom this morning, but the soldiers have no one among them who knows this country, so they chose to remain with the drive until we pass close to the settlement at Natchitoches, and leave us then."

"We can use 'em," Ben said with a nod, then turned when he saw Hacha ride up from the rear of the herd.

The Yaqui reined in beside Ben and said, "Two Comanches scout camp last night. I find sign at first light and follow tracks back to canyon."

Ben thought for a moment before he said, "We have to know if them Indians are comin' after us. Hacha, I want you to stay behind the herd. Day or so back, far 'nough so you can give us warnin' if you see 'em comin'. Take grub for a week, 'n a spare mount in case you got t' get back in a hurry. Uncle Ezra 'n I'll keep watch over things here."

BEN HAD HIS fingers crossed, and he didn't know why. It was the evening of the second day since the herd made an easy crossing at the Trinity River, and everything was going great. The land they traveled through was lush with rich grass and the cattle had put on weight. The longhorns were more manageable now, and making good time on the trail.

He and Uncle Ezra had spent most of the last two days in the saddle, ranging far out to the sides and ahead of the herd, but had seen no sign of Indians or any other kind of trouble. Hacha hadn't been heard from, so the Comanches weren't a threat.

Ben looked up at the night sky. The heavy clouds had stayed with them and they had gotten some rain, but that cooled things off and made travel more comfortable.

Still, he was worried. Ben decided maybe he was just tired and vowed to make sure he got a good night's sleep tonight.

He took care of his horse, then went to the cook wagon for some coffee and a plate of beans. Paco was there and made place beside him on a log for Ben to sit.

Ben slowly chewed his food while he looked around and to find everything peaceful. The cook's helper applied gobs of grease to the big wooden hubs of the cook wagon wheels. That had to be done every two days to prevent wear.

He watched the *vaqueros* throw the dregs of their coffee cup against the side of the canvas that covered the water barrel. Cookie claimed that would keep the contents cooler somehow.

Ben saw something that really puzzled him, so he turned to Paco and asked, "What's that rider doin' over there."

Paco looked where Ben pointed, then smiled and said, "That is a horsehair rope. Very hard to make, but many people believe if they spread such a rope around themselves when they sleep, a snake will not crawl over it."

Ben didn't say anything. He just shook his head and thought about the Comanches burying their dead above ground, then decided you didn't have to be an Indian to have strange beliefs. He finished his meal and decided it was time for bed.

BEN WAS JARRED from his slumber by a clap of thunder so loud he thought it was in bed with him; the sky lit up like it was mid-day when a bolt of lightning shot down out of the dark clouds and enveloped a solitary oak tree between camp and the herd. Ben jumped to his feet in fear.

The blue-white flame struck the uppermost branches of the hundred-year old landmark, then burned its way in a circle around the trunk until it collided with the sandy soil where it scorched the ground in all directions.

Ben was over a hundred yards away, but the force of the impact threw him to the ground. He turned his head to see the tree explode in flame like a giant solitary torch. The cattle came to their feet like a shot and, without a sound, the entire herd took off in an all out dash and stampeded into the dark.

Every man in camp scrambled from bed and pulled on their boots, some didn't even bother with pants, then ran to the remuda for a horse to get after the rampaging animals.

Ben threw a saddle on his stallion, then took off at a gallop, amazed that the long-legged, gangly longhorns could run so fast. The closely bunched cattle raced along, their hooves pounded against the ground and their horns clashed together as they thundered through the night.

Ben looked to his left. Uncle Ezra and Paco charged up beside him and he hollered, "Keep the cattle headed east 'til we can get 'em turned."

They nodded they understood, then all three spurred their horses to try and get in front of the stampeding longhorns.

Ben saw a rider on the far side of the herd go down, but in the dark, he couldn't tell who, then he was in the clear, ahead of the charging horde. He reached behind him and untied his jacket from the saddle, then flapped it in the faces of the steers in the lead.

The wild-eyed longhorns ignored Ben at first, then Paco and Uncle Ezra joined him and the cattle started to slowly veer away from the riders.

Several *vaqueros* caught up to help and the additional men caused the head of the stampede to turn in a wide arc and start to slow.

Ben signaled for the riders to keep the pressure on, and after a couple more miles they finally managed to force the leaders of the herd to circle back into the cattle behind them. He saw several cows go down and get trampled by the hooves of the ones behind. The longhorns milled around and brushed up against each other until they tired out, then the cattle started to settle down and the stampede was over.

Ben rode up beside Paco and said, "Now I know how the Comanches felt the other night. Them longhorns make a fearsome sight when they get to runnin'."

Paco took off his hat to wipe his brow and said, "They are that. The cattle are tired now, but we'll have to ride herd on them for the rest of the night. The longhorns are still nervous and the slightest thing could start them running again."

Ben lifted his face to the sky and realized for the first time it was raining. The thunder and lightning that started the stampede was now far to the east of the herd, but that didn't mean they wouldn't get more.

Ben wheeled his horse around and said, "Take care of things here. I'll check on the wagons."

He passed only a few downed cattle after he left the end of the herd, then ahead of him loomed a pile up of five or six animals. Ben moved closer when he noticed the black and white corpse of a pinto pony among the longhorns, then his worst fears were realized when he spotted a splash of bright yellow.

He dismounted, then turned away at the sight. It was one of the *vaqueros*. Ben couldn't tell who, but there was no doubt the rider was dead. The man's body was smashed almost level with the ground, his face gone. The only identifiable thing left was the yellow vest the man wore and it was now stained with blood.

Ben looked up to see the cook wagon roll to a stop. The cook got down with a lantern and walked to the body. The old man made the sign of the cross, then lowered his head and said, "It is Juan Morales. He had only nineteen years. The vest was a gift from his father."

Ben accepted a cup of coffee from the cook after they wrapped the grisly remains in a blanket and put the body on the wagon, then the cook moved out. The coffee would be needed ahead to keep the *vaqueros* awake throughout the long night.

Ben met the others from camp after another mile on the trail. He rode up to them and asked, "Everybody all right?"

Pilar leaned out of carriage and said, "No one here is injured. Were any of our men hurt?"

"Lost one I know of. Youngster by the name of Juan Morales. Got caught in the stampede."

Pilar was shocked at the news of the man's death. She put her hand to her mouth and said, "Poor Juan. He was little more than a boy."

Ben thought it a little strange when she spoke of Juan as being so young, since Pilar could hardly be much older herself. To comfort her, he said, "He died like a man. We best get on ahead and make camp. There'll be precious little rest for anyone tonight."

The rain was still pelting down when they buried Juan Morales the next morning. There was little to mark that the boy passed this way, other than the crude cross made of sticks that stood at the head of his grave.

Ben left to check the trail ahead after the service. The amount of rain had him worried. It was only a short distance to where they planned to cross the cattle and when he topped the last hill, his worst fears were realized. The Neches River was out of its banks, swollen to three times its normal width and just as deep. Fallen trees and debris bobbed and tumbled in the swirling brown water at an alarming rate of speed.

He had seen enough, and reined his horse around to ride back and tell the others the bad news.

Ben was surprised to find the herd stopped when he arrived, then he noticed Joseph and a group of riders gathered at the wagons. The men stood aside when he rode up and he saw Hacha talking with much gesturing of his arms.

Ben knew of only one reason for Hacha to be here, but he tied off his horse after he dismounted and asked anyway, "Indians?"

The Yaqui nodded his head and said, "Many Comanches come. Catch up tomorrow, or maybe next day."

Joseph turned to Ben and asked, "How far is it to the river? We must get the cattle across and find a place to make a stand."

"Indians ain't our only problem. The Neches's out of its banks, 'n I'm not sure the longhorns can swim to the other side."

"But we must cross," Joseph said. "It is our only chance. Hacha says over a hundred braves are behind us."

Ben shrugged his shoulders, then said, "Then we'll have to find a way."

Chapter Twenty

BEN TOOK HACHA AND EZRA with him to the river. They had to find a way to cross, and fast.

Ezra whistled through his teeth when he saw the raging torrent, then scratched his chin and said, "Don't look good, do it? Must be near a hundred yards 'cross there, 'n fast as that water's movin', cattle wouldn't stand a chance. We'll have t' leave the wagons behind."

Ben said, "We got to figger somethin'," then he turned to Hacha and asked, "Any place you know of that'd be better than here?"

"This is the only crossing for many miles."

Ben thought for a moment, then said, "That means if we get across, a few men'd be able to stop the Indians from usin' the only place they could ford to come after us."

Uncle Ezra said dryly, "That's true, if we was on the other bank, but the river ain't goin' down, 'n I don't see no way for us t' get there, not with the cattle."

Ben studied the scene in front of him, then snapped his fingers and said, "Maybe there's a way."

Hacha and Uncle Ezra looked at the river, then at each other and finally back at Ben. The look on their faces said that if there was a way to get the cattle across, they sure didn't see it.

Ben got down from his horse and knelt on the ground, then picked up a stick and said, "Way I figger, river's only twenty . . . thirty yards wide when it ain't flooded. That's the only part the cows'll have to swim. They can walk most of the way in and out."

Uncle Ezra protested, "Current's too swift for that. Hell, we don't even know if them longhorn's can swim, 'n what about all the stuff in the water. Looks like ever' tree and bush for a hundred miles is floatin' down stream out there."

Ben drew some lines in the sand and said, "Thought about that. We'll put *vaqueros* in the shallows up stream on both sides of the river. The riders'll rope the big trees 'n pull 'em on shore 'fore they get t' the crossing. We can rig several lines into a net 'n tie it across the river to catch the small stuff, 'n have men to clean it out if it starts t' fill up. The longhorns are pretty well trail broke 'n followin' their leaders, so we'll tie ropes on the lead steers, 'n pull 'em across. The rest'll follow."

Ezra looked at the drawing, then at the river and finally said, "Lines in the sand look fine, but how do we know it'll work out there. Seems awful chancy t' me, 'n what about the wagons? You ain't said nothin' 'bout them."

"Won't know for sure, 'til we try it," Ben said. "They need these cattle in Louisiana, 'n if we stay on this side of the river, the Comanches'll get them 'n us too. Might lose a few head this way, but I don't see where we got much choice. As for the wagons, we'll tie big logs to the sides, 'n float 'em 'cross like they was a raft."

Uncle Ezra still looked skeptical, but he said, "'Spect you're right. It's the only chance we got. Least the rain's let up. How're we gonna get the ropes to the other side?"

Ben turned to Hacha and said, "Ride back 'n fill Joseph in on our plans. Have him send some men up here to cut trees. Get some more rope and when you get back take a line across between those two big trees so we can pull the net over. I'll tie the ones we have here together 'n take 'em to the other bank where we'll pull the steers out."

Hacha handed his rope to Ezra before he rode off, while Ben sat down and removed his boots, then skinnied out of his clothes and tied the end of the rope around his bare middle. He unsaddled his stallion, led the horse to the edge of the river, then mounted and, after he checked for floating trees, plunged into the swirling brown water.

His stallion lost its footing and almost went under when they were thirty yards out, then recovered and started to swim strongly for the opposite shore.

Ben let go of the reins and eased over the horse's rump to make it easier for the animal to swim, then grabbed the stallion's tail with both hands and hung on while he was propelled through the churning water.

The current surged against them with such force when they reached the middle of the river that Ben feared not even the great strength of the stallion would be enough to keep them from being sucked under. He felt the horse give a mighty effort and find solid footing with its front hooves, then lunge forward to pull Ben into the shallows.

He scrambled to his feet and led his mount up the bank to dry ground, then looked around to see they'd come out of the river at least a hundred yards downstream from the place they entered on the other side.

Ben sank to the ground, exhausted from the swim. He rested for a few minutes, then got up, patted the stallion on the neck and said, "Good boy. That was close. I'd a never made it without you."

Ben looked across the river to see that Joseph and the others had arrived, so he tied the rope high on the bank to prevent it from snagging objects floating in the river, then signaled he was ready.

Ben waited until Uncle Ezra tied the ends of extra ropes to the one already across, then pulled them to him.

He turned in time to see Hacha guide his mount into the river on the other side. The Yaqui's horse was well out in the water, swimming hard and making good progress, then

Ben spotted an almost submerged log that barreled down from upstream.

He shouted a warning and pointed, but it was no use. Hacha was low in the water clinging to his pony's tail, so Ben knew his friend couldn't see the danger, and it was impossible for Hacha to hear over the sound of the rushing water.

Ben quickly grabbed a rope and ran along the edge of the bank, then waded out in the shallows. He formed a loop on the end of the lariat and made ready to cast it out.

Hacha was over halfway through the heavy current, but Ben could see the Yaqui wasn't going to make it. The log was only yards from the swimming pony.

Ben moved out until water lapped at his waist, then, braced himself against the current, and threw the rope as he yelled, "Turn loose of your pony 'n grab on."

Hacha turned and saw the danger, then released his hold on the horse's tail and gripped the lariat as it settled around his shoulders.

Ben flipped the rope high in the air to get slack so the log could sail under it, then the large chunk of wood crashed into the pinto's chest and drove the wide-eyed animal beneath the churning water.

Ben fought to keep the weight on the end of the lariat from jerking him into the river when Hacha rolled under the surface, then the log slid past and Ben was able to maneuver the Yaqui into the shallows.

Ben grabbed Hacha under the shoulders to pull him from the water, then both men collapsed on the ground and gasped for breath when they reached the bank.

They sucked hard to fill their burning lungs with air for a full five minutes before either man moved.

Ben finally opened his eyes and asked, "Are you hurt?"

"Bruised only, thanks to you, my brother. If you don't throw the rope, I am on the bottom of river with my horse."

Ben got to his feet, clapped his friend on the shoulder and said with a smile, "'Nough of this rest. We got lots to do yet."

He helped Hacha up, then looked across the water and saw Joseph already had men felling trees on the other side, then the first of the cattle topped a ridge not more than half a mile from the river and Ben knew time was running out.

Hacha pointed with his hand and said, "Water goes down."

Ben scratched his chin, then nodded and said, "Not fast enough, but it might make crossin' a little easier. I'll leave my horse here while we get t' the other side."

They secured the rope so it was suspended ten feet above the raging water, then started to work their way, hand over hand, to the other bank.

Ben went first and noticed the wagons were pulled up beside the river as he snaked his way slowly across the rope. He dropped off into the shallow water to wade ashore, then sensed something coming at his head and put his hand up in time to snatch a set of buckskins out of the air.

Ben looked around in confusion and spotted his uncle on the bank with a big grin on his face.

Ezra looked at his nephew and said dryly, "Best shuck into them things, boy, 'fore ya shock the womenfolk."

Ben looked down and felt the heat rise in his neck. The fact he was buck naked had completely slipped his mind and there was no place to hide. He glanced toward the wagons as he scrambled to get into his leather breeches and what he saw there almost caused him to fall over.

Doña Maria was nowhere in sight, but Pilar was there. She stared directly at him from a distance of not more than twenty feet. Pilar stood with her arms folded across her chest and the smile on her face told Ben that she wasn't at all sympathetic to his discomfort.

He hurriedly dressed and pulled on his boots, then walked away without saying a word, but his ears burned as the tinkle of laughter sounded behind him.

Hacha and Ezra joined Ben at the remuda and he noticed that even the normally stoic Indian had a hint of a smile.

Ben decided to just ignore the whole thing. He saddled his roan, then turned and asked, "How long 'til the net 'n wagons are ready?"

Ezra lowered the butt of his rifle to the ground, then said, "Net's made 'n the men'll have the logs tied on by the time we're set t' go."

"Good, I'll put the net in place." Ben said, then he turned to Hacha and continued, "Scout the Comanches 'n see how far away they are. We got to get the wagons across before the main body of cattle get here."

Ezra loosed a stream of brown liquid derived from his ever present plug of tobacco, then said, "Saw how far the current drifted you 'n your horse. Figger we put the long-horns in a hundred yards upstream, they ought t' come out 'bout right on your side."

Ben nodded his agreement, then returned to the river bank. He noticed the water level was down, but not much, so he rode upstream to see how things were going there.

Several large tree trunks were pulled up on the bank on both sides of the river and Ben stopped to watch a *vaquero* snare another.

He saw the rider ease his horse into the shallows until belly deep, then cast his rope out into the river. The loop settled around the branches of a floating tree. The *vaquero* snubbed the lariat to the horn of his saddle and used the strength of his horse to drag the trunk out onto the shore, then loosened his rope and went back, ready for the next one.

Satisfied the *vaqueros* could stop anything large from coming down river, Ben returned to the suspended rope and crossed to the other side to secure the net. This time he made sure he kept his clothes on.

He tied the bottom of the net a foot beneath the surface of the water, with the top of it extending two feet above, then looked across the river and saw the wagons were ready.

Ezra sent the buggy across first, since it was the lightest and would be easier for Ben to handle alone. Men used long poles to propel the logs tied to the buggy, then would help him with the other vehicles when they were across the river.

Ben took his end of a line tied to the front of the make-shift raft and took a turn around a tree for leverage, then took up the slack as the buggy floated out on the water while men on the other shore played out a rope attached to the rear. The swift current in the river pushed hard at the logs and the line almost slipped from Ben's grasp when the vehicle reached midstream. He redoubled his effort and strained against the unending pressure. Ben felt the muscle and sinew in his back threaten to tear, then the buggy floated free of the current and glided through the shallow water to the bank.

Ben lay back and rested while the two men cut the logs free and pulled the buggy on shore, then got up and the three of them brought the freight wagon over without any problem.

He looked back after the cook wagon was safely across and saw the main body of longhorns top the hill that over-looked the river, so he returned to the other side.

Joseph was waiting for him with a worried look on his face and said, "The cattle smell water and are thirsty. My men try to slow them down, but it is not easy."

Ben surveyed the mass of longhorns that milled back and forth on the hill, then said, "Get your lead steers down here and get ropes on 'em, then start drivin' the cattle down. Don't let 'em stop when they get to water. The cows can drink after they're on the other side."

The men on the opposite bank started to pull as soon as the lead steers were in place and the animals plunged into the river with the rest of the longhorns close behind.

Ben saw that they didn't need to worry about the rangy critters ability to swim. The long legged cattle took to the water like ducks. Their movement through the river wasn't pretty, all you could see was the tips of their horns and the ends of their noses, but move they did and in moments the first longhorns emerged from the river and ran up onto the far bank.

Chapter Twenty-One

BEN TOOK OFF HIS HAT and glanced at the sky. The night was clear and the stars were bright as only prairie stars can be. He noted the position of big dipper was almost directly below the north star, so he knew the time was around four in the morning.

Ben gazed out over the sea of longhorns being driven into the water and gave a grim smile. They were going to make it. The crossing had gone well, and in another two hours, or maybe less, the last of the cattle would be on the the far side of the river and out of reach of the Indians.

He turned as Hacha galloped up and slid his pony to a halt.

The Yaqui left his horse on the run, then stopped in front of Ben and said, "The Comanches come."

"How much time we got?"

"Scouts will be here soon. Main body in maybe two hours. They ride fast."

Ben's brow wrinkled in thought, then he said, "Damn, that's gonna be cuttin' it mighty close. 'Spect you 'n me better slow them Indians down some."

They went over to Joseph and Ben said, "Comanches on the way. Hacha 'n me are gonna try to discourage 'em a little. Better get the remuda 'cross now, then if you have to leave anything behind, it'll just be a few head of cattle."

Ezra walked up in time to overhear the conversation and said, "I'll get my gun 'n go with you."

Ben reached out a hand and touched his uncle on the arm and said, "No, you stay here. Anythin' happens to us, they'll need you to get the cattle through. 'Sides, I want you t' get some of those trees we pulled up on the bank 'n build us a barricade on the other side. We're gonna need somethin' t' fight behind if we plan to stop the Indians from comin' across. Leave some men over there to give me 'n Hacha cover. We might be comin' fast, time we get to the crossin'."

"I'll get her done, boy. Don't worry none about that. You just keep a tight hold on your topknot."

"I'll do it, Uncle Ezra. You hear any shootin', get everybody across the river 'n skedaddle with what you got. We'll be along."

Pilar was already across and Ben couldn't say good bye, so he and Hacha took extra rifles, then rode away from the crossing.

They found the perfect place to make their stand twenty minutes after leaving the river. Leaving their horses at the bottom of a ridge, they climbed to the top and got into position.

Ben smiled grimly when he looked down at the trail and saw how the light of the full moon reflected off the white sand and would outline the figures of the Indians if they arrived before dawn.

The two men placed their spare weapons at five foot intervals along the top of the ridge in the hope they could make the Comanches believe they were against a larger number of foes.

Hacha twisted his head toward Ben as two braves appeared below, then turned back when he received a signal to let the riders pass.

Ben didn't want to risk a gunshot for fear of alerting the main body of Indians and the bucks were out of reach of an arrow. He knew it was a risk to let the two braves get between them and the river.

Hacha turned toward Ben as the sound of approaching riders reached the top of the ridge. The pre-dawn tracings of the coming sun had started to streak across the morning sky, and they had a clear view when the band of Comanches suddenly appeared on the trail, over a hundred of them.

Ben studied the warriors as they approached. They wore their hair long, with feathers and beads braided in it, and they had all manner of paint smeared on their faces and bodies, some even with paint on their horses. The braves rode their ponies without benefit of a saddle and controlled their mounts with only a primitive woven hackamore and the pressure of their knees. The Indians were armed with bows and spears. Several had shields made of buffalo hide, but Ben was relieved to see that only a few carried guns.

He drew back the hammer of his rifle and saw out of the corner of his eye that Hacha had done the same, then the Comanches came into range and Ben squeezed the trigger of his weapon. He aimed to disable rather than kill because a wounded man would slow the Indians down more than a dead one.

His shot was true and hit the shoulder of a brave in the lead, then Ben rolled to his right and picked up a second rifle and fired. He heard Hacha's weapons explode as they both continued to move and fire. The noise was earsplitting as they repeated this maneuver until all the rifles were empty.

Ben stared through the smoke as he recharged his weapons, the sudden silence almost as deafening as the explosions had been. The Indians were in full retreat and left seven wounded braves behind them on the ground along with one buck that appeared to be dead.

The Comanches dismounted out of range of the guns and yelled back and forth among themselves.

Ben turned and asked, "You make out what they're sayin'?"

"Young hot bloods want to charge. The older warriors say to come in slow to find out how many of us they face."

Ben grinned and said, "Reckon that's all we can do here. Let's get out of here 'fore they get behind us."

They fired two more shots to slow the Indians down, then made their way back down to their horses.

Ben mounted and started to rein his horse around when he sensed a presence beside him in the rocks. He heard a gunshot as he turned, then dove from his saddle when he spotted an arrow coming at him.

The shaft passed through the area he'd just vacated, then Ben hit the ground in a long roll and came to one knee with his pistol cocked and pointed to his right. He located his attacker and fired before the brave could loose another arrow.

The lead ball struck the Indian full in the chest and the buck landed flat on his back as his life's blood stained the sand around him.

Hacha rode up and said, "The scouts. I shot the second one. Other Comanches will hear shots and come."

Ben vaulted into the saddle and they galloped toward the river. They were barely a hundred yards down the trail when blood curdling screams sounded behind them and Ben looked back to see the first of the Indians boil around the end of the ridge.

He didn't waste time trying to get off a shot, instead, he leaned low in the saddle and urged his horse to greater speed. Ben felt the roan respond beneath him and by the time they topped the ridge that overlooked the crossing, the Comanches were far behind, but still coming hard.

Ben looked ahead and saw that all of their men and horses were on the other side of the river. A small number of longhorns remained on this side, but the animals still entered the water, not wanting to be left behind.

The cattle scattered when Ben and Hacha rode through them to plunge their horses into the river at a dead run. They went off their mounts and hung from their saddles when they reached deep water so the Indians would have a smaller target.

Arrows peppered down around them when they splashed into the shallows. One creased the flank of Hacha's pony, then the Indians were caught by surprise and forced to retreat by a barrage of gunfire that erupted from the logs on the bank.

The withering fire allowed Ben and Hacha to scramble out of the water and they plopped on their bellies behind the crude barricade.

Ezra peered through the smoke and said, "Cut it a mite close, didn't ya boy?"

Ben smiled at his uncle and said, "Couldn't a been closer. Thought you were goin' with the herd?"

"They ain't so far ahead, I can't catch up."

Ben noted the position of the six men with Uncle Ezra, then turned his attention back to the Comanches.

The Indians were gathered well back from the water on the far shore, out of effective musket range. They seemed to argue among themselves, then the entire group of warriors turned as one and raced their ponies toward the river.

The painted Indians brought a chill to the men behind the barricade. The braves rode with weapons brandished above their heads and yelled at the top of their lungs as they guided their horses at a full gallop with their knees so both hands were free to fire arrows.

The warriors hit the crossing in full stride, but when they left the shallow water, their mounts were slowed by the current and the bucks became easy targets for the guns of the men on shore.

Ben fired and saw a brave clutch at his head and go down, then he reloaded and shot again. This time his aim was to kill, not to wound.

Warriors in front went down and their ponies too, then the ones behind plowed into their fallen comrades to create a mass of horse flesh and men that reared and plunged as the bucks struggled to bring their mounts under control.

The thunder of weapons exploding around Ben blotted

out the sound of the dying Indians and horses from his ears, but the smell of blood and gunpowder attacked his nostrils. The men behind the barricade strained to find a target through the murky cloud of smoke that was all around them, then fired and raised more smoke.

Ben settled the sights of his rifle on the broad chest of a Comanche on a pinto pony, then lowered his weapon before he dropped the hammer when the Indians suddenly broke off the charge and splashed back toward the far bank.

The firing around Ben ceased as the war party rode out of range, then he looked at the carnage in front of him. He didn't know how many times he'd fired, or any of the others for that matter, but close to twenty riderless horses galloped away with the Comanches when they retreated.

Ezra squirted a stream of tobacco juice at the ground, then said, "Burned 'em good, 'n that's a fact. Think they'll hit us again or ya reckon they had enough?"

Ben leaned his rifle against the logs, then stood up and said, "Hard to say with Indians, but I doubt they'll come at us here. Not with the river up, 'n they got no place else to cross. That the way you see it, Hacha?"

"Comanches lose many warriors. When water go down, they will come."

Ben thought for a moment, then said, "'Spect you're right. Indians still got more men than us, by about four to one, and what's worse, they know it. They hit the herd while we're on the move, they'd wipe us out for sure."

"Water ain't gonna stay up forever," Ezra said. "Startin' to fall now, 'n when it does, this place'll be swarmin' with Comanches."

Ben nodded his head and said, "They can't get across 'til the river's back in it's banks, not with us here, 'n I figger that'll be 'nother day 'n a half, maybe two. The cattle ought to be 'cross the Sabine River and into Louisiana by then. Hacha, you go after the herd 'n keep it movin'. We'll hold the Indians here long as we can, then catch up."

* * *

EZRA CAME UP to Ben just after dusk two nights later and said, "Water's fallin' fast. This ain't gonna be no healthy place t' be, come mornin', 'n them bucks might decide t' come visit 'fore then."

The Indians had tried to sneak across under cover of darkness the night before, but Ben had anticipated that and piled stacks of brush along the shore that he set on fire when the warriors made their move. The light from the burning brush and the fact that the night was clear from an almost full moon caused the Comanches to call off their attack. Indians didn't like to fight at night, and he didn't think they'd try again in the dark, but Uncle Ezra was right. They needed to be gone by morning, so Ben said, "'Spect we better sashay out a here while it's still dark. Have the men bank the fires so they'll burn all night. Use *sombreros* 'n rig some dummies, then place 'em behind the barricade where parts o' the hats show. Tell the men no noise, none. Don't even saddle the horses 'til we're back in the trees. Soon's it's full dark, we'll sneak off. If the Indians are fooled and don't attack 'til dawn, we'll get ourselves a few hours head start."

Ben watched his uncle walk away, then turned his attention to the other side of the river. The fires of the Comanches camp were clearly visible to him. He toyed with the idea of running their pony herd off, then put it out of his mind.

If the Indians thought it was too easy to cross the river, they might come over before Uncle Ezra and the men had a chance to get away.

Ben went to help the others get ready, and the small party was on the trail in less than two hours. They rode hard throughout the night and into the next day before Ben called a halt at noon.

He refilled Ezra's coffee cup and said, "You best drop back behind us a ways. Don't have a spare mount for you, so ride easy 'n rest your horse so he'll be ready to run if you spot the Comanches. We ought to reach the Sabine River 'fore dark. You ain't spotted any savages by then, come join us."

Chapter Twenty-Two

BEN LED THE WAY TO the east after Uncle Ezra turned back. He figured they were home free, so he didn't push the men very hard. They were all pretty done in from the tension of the last few days, and any rest they could get in the saddle would do them all good.

They rode for three hours, then topped a hill and Ben was so surprised by what he saw, he almost fell off his horse. The valley below him was filled with grazing longhorns. The herd wasn't across the Sabine where it should be, hell, it wasn't even on the move. He searched for signs of trouble, then spotted the wagons drawn up on the far side of the cattle and laid his rifle across the fork of his saddle as he led his men down the hill at a gallop.

Ben slid his pony to a stop and dismounted in a cloud of dust, then stepped down in front of Joseph and asked, "What's goin' on here? Why're you stopped? You ought to be on the other side of the river by now."

Joseph held his arms out to his side and said, "We can not go on."

"Why in hell not," Ben demanded. "Comanches're gonna be crawlin' up our backsides anytime now. We got to get movin'."

"It is Ramon Padilla. He has blocked our path to the crossing."

Ben snorted, not believing what he was heard, then said, "You let that pop-n-jay stop you. He can't have more' n a handful of men. We can ride right over 'em."

Joseph shook his head and said, "You do not understand. Ramon went to the outpost at *El Fuerte del Cibolo* and has the entire garrison from the fort with him, over twenty men. The lieutenant from the fort brought me word that we could not cross and demanded our surrender. But that is not the real problem."

Ben scratched his chin, then grumbled, "Sounds pretty good for starters. What else?"

"The men with Ramon are soldiers of the King of Spain, as are my men and I. You must see that it is impossible for us to kill soldiers who only obey orders issued by our king."

"See your problem, but I ain't gonna surrender to Padilla or anybody else. We've gone through too much to get these longhorns to Galvez so he can start his campaign against the British, and I aim t' see he gets 'em."

Joseph screwed his face up in anguish, then said, "I will talk to Ramon. Perhaps I can cause him to change his mind."

Ben walked up beside Joseph's horse after the man was mounted and said, "Don't be long. The Comanches can't be more' n a few hours behind us. If they attack where we are now there's a good chance the longhorns'll stampede right over the top of those boys at the river 'n take care of our problem for us."

Joseph looked startled and said, "We can not allow that to happen. The soldiers would not have a chance."

Ben smiled grimly, then said, "Wouldn't be nothin' we could do about it. I'm gonna move the wagons, just in case. Tell Padilla he don't get his men out of there, it's on his head."

Pilar stepped down from her carriage after Joseph left. She overheard the conversation and had a look of concern on her face.

She walked up to Ben and gripped his arm, then said, "I know how strong you feel about this thing, but surely you don't believe it is more important than the lives of the men at the river?"

"Out of my hands. Soldiers down there are Padilla's problem. If the Indians cause the longhorns to run in that direction, nothin' I can do about it."

She stamped her foot on the ground and said, "You want a stampede don't you? What about Joseph? He is your friend and it's not fair for you make him choose between his loyalty to the King and this mission of yours."

Ben took Pilar's hands in his, then stared deep into her eyes for a moment before he said, "Fair don't have nothin' to do with it. The colonies, my people, are in a war that'll decide if we live as free men, by our own laws, or be crushed under the harsh rule of the British. These longhorns could make the difference. No man, or group of men, is bigger to me than that, so whatever it takes, I'm gonna get the cattle through."

"Yes, but," she started to say, then Ben interrupted, "You told me one time about how your daddy and others from the old country would have to change to become a part of this new land. That's what we're fightin' for, the right to change 'n grow as a people. To me, that's something worth fighting for, 'n dying too, if need be.

"Don't worry about the soldiers at the crossin'. Joseph's gonna tell Padilla how things stand. He'll move his men out. He's got to, 'n when he does, I'm takin' the longhorns to the other side the river."

Pilar studied him for a moment, then said, "If you are sure none of the soldiers will be injured, I will help."

He took her face between his hands and felt the smooth texture of her skin as he said, "I promise you this. Nobody'll get hurt . . . unless they try to stop me. Now, let's get your buggy 'n the wagons moved out o' the way. You hear any shootin', head for the river. I'll get Paco 'n some *vaqueros* to stay with you."

Hacha rode up to join Ben once the wagons were situated and they sat on their horses to watch for any activity down by the river, but nothing was going on down there yet.

The Yaqui turned and asked, "What do we do now?"

"You, me 'n Uncle Ezra, when he gets here, are gonna set up west of the herd. If Padilla don't see things our way, we'll wait 'til he moves his men, then stampede the long-horns across the river. That is, if the Comanches give us the chance. The Indians attack 'fore we're ready, we'll just keep the cattle movin' in the right direction."

"What did Joseph think of your plan?"

Ben looked at Hacha and said, with a grim smile on his face, "Not sure. He don't rightly know about it just yet."

Hacha pointed toward the river and said, "Maybe now is a good time to find out what he thinks."

They turned to watch, through a cloud of dust, the column of men that rode in their direction. Joseph was beside Padilla and behind them trailed the soldiers from the garrison.

Padilla was mad as a hornet when he stopped his horse in front of Ben and demanded, "How dare you threaten soldiers of the king while on Spanish soil?"

Ben noticed Padilla's twenty men spread out to encircle the two of them and eased his mount to the right so the barrel of his rifle was centered between the gold buttons that adorned the captain's chest, then slowly said, "Hold it right there, *Capitán*. Didn't say I'd stampede the cattle. Just sent you word what would happen if the Indians did attack. Your men would of been in a bad way, where you had 'em."

Paco and a group of *vaqueros* rode up, attracted by the commotion, then sat immobile on their horses. Ben glanced briefly in their direction and saw indecision on their faces as to what their role was in this.

Mad at the fact that his decision was being questioned in front of others, Padilla sputtered, "That is not the way I see it. In any case, you are breaking Spanish law. That makes you an enemy of Spain. It is my duty place you under arrest and arrange transportation to Mexico City for trial."

Ben looked at Joseph's face and saw the anguish there, but no firm resolve. Hacha was ready but Ben knew the two of them had no chance with the odds ten to one against them in close quarters.

He also didn't plan on going to some Spanish prison while the politicians sorted things out, so he raised the barrel of his rifle slightly and tensed his muscles, but before he could speak, Pilar arrived.

She rode into the cluster of horsemen, then stopped her mount between the two sides and Ben realized he'd lost his chance. He couldn't start anything and risk her being hurt.

Pilar's eyes flashed fire when she said, "Stop this insanity. Ramon Padilla, you have known me and my family for years, as well as Joseph and the rest of the people here. There can be no doubt of our loyalty to Spain, and if we did not believe that what we do is in the best interest of the crown, we would not be doing it."

Taken aback by the verbal assault, Padilla said stubbornly, "It is against Spanish law to transport cattle from one province to another."

Joseph said, "As I told you, Ramon, Governor Galvez has requested permission to import longhorns into Louisiana. He needs them as food for his troops when Spain declares war on England. We know the transfer will be approved, and in fact, the notice may have already been posted. Think carefully of your motives. If you deny the cattle to our troops, you will seriously hinder the Spanish war effort."

Padilla drew himself up straight in the saddle and said, "I must follow my orders."

The Texas sun beat down on Ben's back and he could feel the sweat soak through his shirt, but he figured the talking was over, so he nodded to Hacha and they started to ease their way to the side. He hoped to take Padilla's men by surprise and reach the back of the herd to stampede the cattle across the river, but it didn't look good. Their every move was covered by Spanish guns.

Before any action could be taken, a sentry called out, "Riders approach from the west."

Ben turned to see a column of Spanish soldiers, headed by Uncle Ezra, ride up the trail. "Just what I need," he mumbled to himself, then let his muscles relax to await this latest development.

He glanced sideways and was amazed to see Joseph turn to meet the new arrivals with a big smile on his face.

Ezra stopped his pony, then jumped from the saddle and said, "Comanches comin', big bunch of 'em, 'bout an hour back. Picked up these boys on the way in. Why'n hell is the herd stopped here?"

"Tell you about it later," Ben said, then he reined his horse close to Padilla and asked, "What'd you say? We don't move now, we'll lose the cattle."

"We will engage the hostiles here. What happens to the cattle is not my concern, but it is still against the law to move them across the river and that will not be permitted."

Joseph walked up, accompanied a man from the column and said, "May I present Francisco Garcia, Special Emissary to the government from Governor Galvez. Francisco is an old friend and has news that may solve all our problems."

"What news?" Padilla asked skeptically.

"Spain officially declared war against England on May 8th, and came out in full support of the American colonies struggle for freedom," Joseph said, excitedly. "More than that, Francisco carries authorization signed by Teodoro de Croix, Commandant General of New Spain, for Governor Galvez to be given as many cattle as he needs to wage war against the British."

Padilla examined the documents at length, then raised his eyes from the papers and looked at Joseph.

Ben could tell the man didn't like the idea, but finally Padilla said, "It seems I no longer have authority to prevent transport of longhorns to Louisiana. My soldiers will set up a defensive position here to guard against an attack by the Comanches while you cross the river."

Joseph looked up at Ben with relief and asked, "Should we stampede the cattle?"

"Not if we can help it. I'll get the wagons over first. Have your *vaqueros* get the longhorns on the move. Tell 'em to ride loose in the saddle, 'n be on the lookout for any stray Indians. Most of the riders need to hang back to the rear of the herd. If the Indians break through, or somehow get around the soldiers, then our only choice'll be to stampede 'em."

Ben took Hacha and Uncle Ezra with him to relieve the *vaqueros* with the wagons, then whipped the horses in a mad dash toward the crossing. The Sabine was well within its banks when they arrived and the vehicles and fully a third of the cattle had splashed safely to the other shore before they heard the sound of shots break out behind the herd. First a ragged few, then a crescendo that swelled until it echoed like thunder.

Ben pulled Uncle Ezra aside and said, "Rig us some cover on this side. If we have to fight them Comanches again, reckon this's good a place as any. Me 'n Hacha'll wander back 'n see how things 're going, maybe whittle the odds down a mite."

They circled wide around the herd to come out in the hills on the far side of the barricade the soldiers had thrown up.

Ben climbed a tall pine tree to observe the battle. The Indians milled just out of musket range to draw fire from the defenders, then raced in to loose their arrows. The soldiers were holding their own, Ben decided as he watched, then he caught movement out of the corner his eye. A band of warriors, twenty or thirty strong, were moving through a deep gully. The gash in the earth hid the Comanches from the view of the men behind the barricade and came out to the rear of the soldiers. If the bucks surprised the defenders, it could turn into a massacre.

Ben shinnied down the tree and told Hacha the situation, then they moved to a hill that overlooked where the warriors would come out of the gully. They waited until the Indians were free of the draw and had started to sneak up on the barricade, then opened fire.

Ben's first shot knocked a buck with a fancy headdress on his face in the dirt. He heard Hacha's weapon explode and saw another Comanche fall, then they both fired their rifles as fast as they could recharge the weapons.

The Indians were caught off guard, and the withering fire from the two men dropped four warriors before they knew where the shots came from. The remaining braves started a half-hearted charge up the hill toward Ben and Hacha, but shots from the now alerted soldiers at the barricade peppered the braves and the Indians beat a retreat down the ravine.

The Comanches in front of the barricade also broke off the battle and the fight was over.

Ben and Hacha mounted their horses and rode down to where Padilla waited.

The little captain drew himself up and said grudgingly, "Your help was appreciated."

Ben gave a little bow and said, "As was yours, *Capitán*."

Padilla smiled slightly, then said, "You should have no further problems. The worst is over."

Ben wheeled his horse to ride back to the river, then gave a wave of his hand and said, "Hope you're right."

Chapter Twenty-Three

BEN SAT AND WATCHED THE last of the longhorns splash out of the water and trot ashore on the Louisiana side of the river. The muscles of the horse beneath him trembled with fatigue and Ben looked up at the moonlit sky to see the time was a little after midnight.

He sucked in a lung full of the clean night air, then dismounted and unsaddled his horse. He turned the stallion over to the wrangler and was attracted to the cook fire by the fragrant aroma of boiling coffee

He squatted down to pour himself a cup, then took a sip and turned to Joseph. "Men are tired, animals too. Ought to be safe enough for us to lay over for a day or so 'n let 'em get rested up."

Joseph seemed to hesitate for a moment before he said, "I suppose we must stop, but it is of great importance that I be in New Orleans by the middle of the month."

"First time I heard about a date," Ben said thoughtfully, then added, "You got near on to two weeks 'til then. What happens on the fifteenth?"

Joseph seemed to try and brush it off by turning away as he said, "Oh, nothing, really. A ship from Spain is due to arrive, and on board are a number of things I must transport to my *rancho*."

Ben wondered briefly why Joseph was being so vague, but didn't inquire further, instead he emptied the remains

181

of his coffee in the fire and said, "Think I'll turn in."

The camp was alive with activity by the time Ben rolled out of his blankets the next morning. He stretched to loosen his tired muscles, then strapped on his pistol belt and walked down to the river.

Ben sat down on the bank next to his uncle, then tossed a stone into the water to watch the ripples it created.

Uncle Ezra lazed back against a tree. He looked over and said, "Right smart idea, this takin' a day off. This here life'd be right easy t' get used to."

"Must be old age settin' in," Ben said, as a slight grin tugged at the corners of his mouth.

Ezra bolted up from the ground like a shot, then gave a snort and said, "Listen t' me, buster, some things're better with age. I'm like a fine wine, that's what. Just get better ever' year that passes."

Ben clapped his uncle on the shoulder and said, "Glad to hear it, 'cause I got a job for you."

"If ya think it's somethin' an old man can do, reckon I can give it a shot. What's botherin' you, boy?"

He smiled at his uncle's sarcasm, then said, "Joseph sent a rider to New Orleans yesterday to let the governor know we're in Louisiana with the longhorns. He'll send an escort, 'n I want you to scout the trail we'll be drivin' the cattle down 'til you meet up with 'em, then get the soldiers back to camp fast as you can."

Ezra looked at his nephew and asked, "You expect more trouble from the Indians? Hell, boy, we sent them packin' with their tails 'tween their legs. They ain't gonna be back."

"Ain't Comanches I'm worried 'bout. The British got wind of us goin' to Texas 'fore we left, now that war's been declared, I don't figger they forgot. Way we been thinkin' about nothin' but Indians, the Redcoats could've been stalkin' us 'n know where we are. Got me a bad feelin'. Could be wrong, but I'm gonna scout east of here 'n check it out."

* * *

BEN STOPPED ON a ridge that overlooked the river to give his horse a blow and stared through the twilight haze at the cattle below. Something wasn't right. He'd expected to meet the herd down trail a ways. When they weren't there, Ben backtracked to find the longhorns still grazing where he left them two days ago.

He'd ridden halfway to the Mississippi, and although there was sign of men and horses moving through the area, he hadn't actually seen any Redcoats. Still, Ben was worried.

The cloak of darkness settled around him as he nudged his mount in the ribs and picked his way down the ridge, then reined up to answer the challenge of a sentry.

He didn't know the two Spanish soldiers on guard, so he said, "I'm Ben Cross. You some of the men sent by Galvez to guard the herd?"

"*Si*, Governor Galvez send us," came the reply, then the sentries moved aside to let him pass.

Ben dismounted and tied his horse to the wagon, then walked to where his uncle and Joseph were talking to a Spanish officer.

Ezra turned toward Ben and asked, "Run into trouble out there, did ya?"

"Nary a bit, just sign. What's goin' on here? Why ain't the herd on the move?"

Ezra squirted a stream of tobacco juice in the dust, then said, "Waitin' for you t' get back. Been a change of plans."

Joseph grabbed Ben's hand and said, "I'm glad you are here," then he motioned to the man beside him and said, "May I present *Capitán* Luis Alvarez. Luis is in charge of the detachment that guards the cattle and has brought great news, along with new instructions for us."

Ben shook the man's hand, then asked, "What news?"

The *capitán* drew himself up to attention and said, "It is my very great honor to inform you that Governor Galvez, on the twenty-seventh of August, launched a successful assault on the British garrison at Fort Bute on the Mississippi. Fort Bute is now under Spanish control."

Ben clapped the man on the shoulder and said, "That was more' n a week ago, and great news it is. The governor didn't waste any time gettin' the war started, did he?"

"No sir, he did not," Luis said, then added, "Preparation for the campaign was complete by the time Governor Galvez received word that war was declared—an army of over fourteen hundred men and a flotilla of four vessels was used to take the Fort."

Uncle Ezra whistled through his teeth, then said, "That's a sizable army for these parts."

Luis nodded his head and said, "Yes, and not only that, thousands more soldiers are on their way from Spain by ship."

Ben said, "Governor's gonna need lots a beef. What's he want us to do?"

"Governor Galvez instructs you to split the herd and take three hundred head to Fort Bute where he is planning the campaign to take the British Fort at Baton Rouge. He will need the beef if the siege is a long one. My men and I are to accompany the rest of the cattle, and the bulls for breeding, to pastures near New Orleans."

Ben thought for a minute, then drew Joseph off to one side and said, "Uncle Ezra 'n I'll take the cattle to Fort Bute. It's not more'n a three or four day drive, so we can pack our supplies on horseback, 'n won't need many men."

Hacha walked up and said, "I will go with you."

Ben put his hand on the Yaqui's shoulder and said, "I want you with me, but Paloma can't come. You must send her to New Orleans. An army camp is no place for a woman."

"Paloma is not like other women."

Ben said firmly, "That's the way it's got to be."

Hacha's eyes grew steely, then he slowly nodded his head, so Ben turned back to Joseph and said, "You take the main herd and wagons on to New Orleans. That'll get you to town in plenty of time to meet the ship with your goods on it, 'n make sure the women're safe at the same time."

Ben thought Joseph had a strange look on his face when he agreed to the plan, but ignored the feeling and left to get ready to leave for Fort Bute.

He let Uncle Ezra pick the men to take with them and Ben had just finished his check of the supplies they would need when Pilar moved swiftly around the end of the wagon, planted herself in front of him and said, "Joseph told me of your plans. I wish to go with you."

Ben looked down into her upturned face then shook his head and said, "No. Wouldn't be safe. Where I'm goin' is a war zone. Ain't no women in a battle camp, except camp followers, 'n you sure ain't one of those."

She asked demurely, "What is a camp follower?"

Ben stared at her for a moment, then stammered, "It's a . . . they're a . . . wives 'n girl friends of the soldiers that a . . . tail along 'n wait in a separate camp when their men go to fight."

"Why do the women do that?"

Ben wasn't crazy about the direction this conversation was headed and he said, "They're there to a . . . comfort their men, 'n, I guess, to treat 'em if they get wounded."

"That is what I want to do for you."

Ben grabbed her by the shoulders and sputtered, "Impossible. I won't hear of it. Your goin' to New Orleans where you'll be safe, 'n that's the end of it."

Pilar lifted her hands to his face and said softly, "*Mi amor*, I know we have not had a chance to speak of it on the drive, but you must understand a thing. You are my man and I am your woman for as long as you wish it to be so. I am not a dainty, shrinking violet of a girl. I am a woman born in this new country and of this new world. I know you are a brave man and have seen you do battle, but the thought of you going into danger without me is more than I can stand. I want to fight at your side, and if you love me as I love you, I must be permitted to accompany you."

Ben looked down at the fiercely determined face and felt his heart give a flutter, then he took her in his arms and said, "It's 'cause I love you that you can't go. You must be where you'll be safe, 'n I promise once we take the Fort at Baton Rouge, I'll come to New Orleans 'n we'll be married."

Pilar went up on tip toe and gave Ben a long kiss, then stepped back and said, "I bow to your wishes, *mi amor.* Conquer the fort with great speed. Joseph has a house in New Orleans. I will await your return there."

She added, with a twinkle in her eye, "I will not tell you to be careful. Your thoughts of our honeymoon will keep you safe," then she turned and said, "I go now before I cry."

Ben watched Pilar's trim figure retreat into the darkness, his thoughts definitely not on war or fighting, then loaded the pack animals, mounted his horse and rode out of camp.

They pushed the small herd at a fast pace, since Ben wasn't sure when the attack on Baton Rouge would begin and reached the Mississippi in three days. The longhorns were easy to move, once they smelled water, because the last two days of the drive had been dry and the cattle were thirsty.

The river was well within its banks and Hacha located a place to swim the herd across a few miles down stream from Fort Bute, but it was nearly dark by the time the last longhorn splashed ashore on the far bank.

Ben pulled his horse up beside Ezra and said, "Bring the cattle along slow once they're watered. I'll ride ahead 'n see the governor; get him to send some men back for the herd."

"I'm ready to turn these damn longhorns over t' somebody," Ezra grumbled. Another week o' this, 'n I'd a sworn off eatin' beef all togather. 'Sides, I'm gettin' tired of havin' t' fix my own grub."

"I'll have the *cantina* staked out for ya," Ben promised, then gigged his stallion in the ribs and rode toward the fort.

Ben brushed the dust from his clothes and removed his hat, then went inside the command post, walked up to the orderly and said, "Like to see Governor Galvez. Name's Ben Cross."

The soldier said, "*Si, Señor* Cross. You are expected," then rose to his feet and opened a door for Ben.

He entered the office to find Oliver Pollock with Galvez.

Both men rose and Galvez, with a big smile on his face, held out his hand and said, "My congratulations to you, sir, on a job well done. A rider brought news of your impending arrival. May I offer you a drink?"

"Thank you, a drink'd be fine, but first I'd like to get somebody to go out 'n relieve my men with the herd."

"Certainly," the governor said, then went to the door and issued the necessary orders to the soldier outside.

Oliver handed Ben a glass of amber liquid and said, "I believe whiskey is your drink of choice, and may I also say the Continental Congress owes you a debt of gratitude for getting the longhorns through. The British will be forced to commit troops to defend their interests in the west against the Spanish and that may be the thing that will turn the war for independence in our favor."

Galvez sat back down and said, "A magnificent undertaking. Did you run into any unforeseen difficulties?"

Ben took a sip of his drink and felt the liquid warm his insides all the way down to his stomach. The oaken taste of the liquor made his mouth tingle and he felt his muscles start to relax. He filled them in on the sequence of events endured to get the cattle through, then he lifted his glass to his lips and after another drink, said, "'Bout what we figgered. Had some good men with me, 'n they made the difference. It was a close thing 'n we were lucky the approval to transport the cattle arrived in time, or I don't know if we'd o' made it. How goes the war back in the colonies?"

Oliver said, "Our soldiers have acquitted themselves valiantly on numerous occasions, and although the inexperience and stupidity of some of our generals cost us early victories, our leadership is now sound and the Continental Army starts to gain the upper hand. We would be winning the war now if it were not for the thousands of mercenary Hessians the British pay to fight for them. Now that Spain has opened a new front here in the west, we can overcome those numbers."

Chapter Twenty-Four

GOVERNOR GALVEZ REFILLED THEIR GLASSES, and his eyes sparkled when he said, "The beef you brought will insure that my army will be well fed, and soldiers with full stomachs always make better fighters.

"I have received a royal decree from my king to drive the British forces out of Pensacola and Mobil in Florida, as well as the posts they occupy along the Mississippi River.

"My troops are well trained, eager for battle, and managed to capture English posts on the Amite River and Thomson's creek even while the main body of my army camped here to recover from the eleven day forced march that allowed us to take Fort Bute."

Ben was impressed and said, "Three victories this fast, that's an unbelievable start."

"Yes, but I fear the challenge that faces us next will be much more formidable. The timing of your arrival is most fortuitous for our purposes, Mr. Cross. I have further need of your services."

"What'd you have in mind?"

The governor unrolled a map on the desk and said, "Baton Rouge is the main source of supply for British armies that fight in the north against George Rogers Clark. If the fort can be captured before winter, we would sever that route and severely hamper the English war effort in that area. I have sent a detachment of soldiers to disrupt communications between Baton Rouge and the British army at Natchez. My men are rested and tomorrow we march on the fort at Baton Rouge."

Ben nodded his head, although he did not yet understand his part in all this as the governor continued, "Some of the Redcoats escaped from Fort Bute, so the British know we are on our way, and my intelligence officer informs me that we will face a seasoned garrison of nearly six hundred men. They have more cannon than we and, not only that, the fort is protected by high palisade walls and surrounded by a ditch eighteen feet wide by nine feet deep. A frontal assault would be suicide for my men, but if we do not come up with a way to breech the walls, and are forced to lay siege to the fort, it could be a very long winter campaign and cost us valuable time."

Ben drained his drink, then sat the glass down and said, "Looks like a tough nut to crack, all right. But, I'm not a military man. What can I do?"

"The fort is a five-day march from here. I want you to lead a patrol to scout the area and try to locate a weakness in the fortifications. The way you used the longhorns to defeat a superior force of Indians leads me to believe you know more about strategy than you realize."

Ben unlimbered his body from the chair and said, "See what I can do, but I'll only need Uncle Ezra 'n Hacha."

Galvez raised an eyebrow and inquired, "Hacha?"

"Yaqui Indian I met in Texas. We couldn't of got the cattle through without him."

Governor Galvez placed his finger on the map and said, "I see, an Indian. Well, as you wish. I will unload my cannon from the boats at this point, a mile and a half this side of our objective. You must meet me there by September twentieth with your report."

* * *

THE MEN FROM the herd rode up as Ben emerged from the headquarters building.

Ezra waved his hand and hollered out, "Where's the *cantina*, boy? I'm so dry, my tongue thinks it's livin' in a desert."

Ben smiled and said, "Don't know, but find us one, 'n the drinks are on me."

They rode up in front of an adobe brick structure that promised liquid refreshment and dismounted.

Ben started inside, then stopped when he noticed Hacha start to walk away.

He moved over to the Yaqui and asked, "You do not join us, brother?"

Hacha looked at Ben and said, "That is not allowed?"

"'Course it is. Come on," Ben said, then grabbed Hacha's arm and led him through the door.

Silence settled over the room and all eyes followed them when they joined Ezra and the riders at a back table.

Ben gave a hard stare at the other people in the tavern and watched in satisfaction as most turned their heads away, then sat down and asked Ezra, "Ordered yet?"

"On the way. Englishman who owns the place claims to have beer cool as a mountain stream."

The burly bartender arrived and placed a glass of foamy dark liquid in front of every man at the table, except Hacha, then stood there with his hands crossed in front of him.

Ben felt a knot of anger ball up in his stomach. He pushed his beer over to Hacha, then looked up with a grim smile and said, "Seems like we're one short."

The bartender said in a gruff voice, "Ye best pay your tab, then drink up and get out. I don't serve redskins."

Ben studied the grimy Englishman. He was a big one, a head taller and broader than any man in the room, with huge shoulders that sloped from a thick neck and a belly that lapped over the front of his belt.

Ben looked up, his eyes hard as stone, and said, "My friends 'n I just want to have a beer. Now, go over there like a good fellow 'n get us another, 'n there won't be no trouble."

The bartender gave a harsh laugh, put his hands on his hips and said, "Trouble—you threaten big Rafe with trouble? Drink up and leave. I don't want your business."

Ben came out of his chair like a shot, intertwined the fingers of both hands in the matted hair of Rafe's head, then slammed the big man's face down into the hard oak surface of the table.

The suddenness of the attack shocked the entire room.

Rafe's nose snapped like a dry twig, and when Ben raised the bartender's head, blood spurted to the floor and the man's eyes were rolled back in his head.

Ben walked Rafe over behind the bar, propped the man against the plank top and said, "Another beer, if you please."

Nobody made a move to interfere while the big man wobbled over to the barrel and returned with a full glass that he placed on the bar.

Rafe must be a real popular man, Ben thought to himself, then he placed coins on the counter and returned to the table where they finished their beer without further interruption.

BEN TOPPED THE ridge overlooking the fort at Baton Rouge just before twilight two days later, with Uncle Ezra and Hacha beside him.

They dismounted and made coffee, then Ben said, "Governor wants us to find a way to take the fort in a hurry, without havin' to lay siege."

Ezra asked, "What exactly are we lookin' for?"

"Don't know for sure, guess anything could be important. The British'll have patrols out, 'n we got two days 'fore the boats'll be here, so I figger we can get into position tonight, 'n each of us scout the fort from a different side during the day, then come back here."

Hacha nodded his head and asked, "Where do you want me?"

"Take the east side, the one with all the trees. I'll scout west; Uncle Ezra, you go north. We'll meet after sundown tomorrow."

THE BOATS WERE docked and the cannon being unloaded by the time they arrived at the river. They rode through the Spanish army spread out along the bank at breakfast, and made their way to the command tent.

Governor Galvez came out to greet them and said, "Good, you are here. I am eager to learn what you have discovered. Dismount and come inside. We will eat and then talk."

The steward poured coffee all around, then Ben said, "Not hungry, Governor. Get your map out 'n we'll bring you up to date on the fortifications."

The diagram of the fort was spread out on the table and Ben marked the locations of the cannon, then said, "Everything's pretty much the way you told me. High wall 'n deep ditch all the way around, the English have livestock 'n supplies inside the enclosure—looks like they're set for a long fight. A drawbridge on the Baton Rouge side of the enclosure covers the gates when it's up. Works on some kind of pully system."

The governor interrupted, "Can the bridge be disengaged?"

"Not from outside the walls. Works're all on the inside. Counted eighteen cannon. Strange the way they placed 'em though. As you can see, eight protect the east wall, four each on the north and south, but only two on the west side."

Galvez leaned over the map, studied it for a moment and said, "They prepare for an assault from the east then?"

"Way I figger it," Ben said. "Might be, the British could of outsmarted themselves."

The governor stared at Ben and said, "You did find a weakness in the defenses then."

Ben shook his head and said, "There's not any real weak spot, 'n I don't know if it'll work, but I got an idea how we might fool the Redcoats."

The governor pursed his lips, then returned to his chair with a slight smile tugging at the corners of his mouth. He crossed his fingers in front of his face, then leaned back and said, "Tell me of your plan, Mr. Cross."

"'Preciate it if you'd call me Ben. Now, this grove of trees on the east side is the only cover in musket shot range of the walls, 'n the obvious place to rush the fort from. The English know that, 'n I think we ought to convince 'em that's just what we're gonna do."

The governor asked, "How will that help us?"

Ben countered with a question. "You got some men that can hit what they aim at with those big guns?"

"Certainly, I number among my soldiers some of the best cannoners in the world. Why do you ask?"

"Tonight, under cover of darkness, send half your men into the woods. Have 'em cut down trees, throw up breast-works, fire on the fort 'n make as much noise as possible—do everything to make the English believe you're going to attack from the trees in the mornin'.

"I'll lead the other half of your soldiers to a place I found on the west side of the fort. We'll build cover for the cannon 'n your men, real quiet-like, then open up on the fort from a hundred yards away at first light. If we do all this without bein' discovered, 'n your men are good as you say, they ought to be able to knock out the British cannon 'fore the Redcoats know what hit 'em."

The governor leaned forward to study the diagram, then nodded his head and said, "It might work, it just might. If we are very convincing with our deception, the English could possibly move additional guns to the east wall during the night

"Only way I can see to keep from having to lay siege to the fort. Depends on if we can fool 'em or not."

"Your plan is a good one, Mr. Cross . . . ah, Ben. I will issue the necessary orders immediately."

BEN SMILED AS he and his uncle sat in the shade and watched the British officers come out to surrender the fort.

Ezra spit a stream of tobacco juice to the ground and said, "Couldn't a gone any slicker."

Ben thought back over the day's events and couldn't agree more. The English bought the idea of an assault from the east, and bombarded the woods with cannon fire throughout the night. The Redcoats didn't discover the real attack until the well barricaded batteries on the west side of the fort opened up at daybreak, and by then, it was too late. The Spanish fire was deadly accurate, as Governor Galvez told Ben it would be, and most of the British cannon were put out of commission in the first few minutes of battle.

The bombardment continued until mid-afternoon when the Commandant of the fort lowered the English flag in defeat. Governor Galvez demanded, and received, not only the unconditional surrender of the troops at Baton Rouge, but also that of the British garrison at Natchez.

Ben turned to Uncle Ezra and said, "Looks like they're about done. Let's go talk to the governor."

They walked into the command tent and found Galvez in a jovial mood. He poured them all a drink, then raised his glass and said, "A toast to you, Ben. Your plan was a stroke of genius and succeeded beyond my wildest dreams."

Ben smiled and said, "I'll drink to that. We caught 'em by surprise, but it was the skill of your cannoners that made the difference, 'n I think they deserve a lot of the credit."

"Granted, and those soldiers will receive commendations, and perhaps promotions. The important thing is that this part of New Spain is now secure, and I am able to proceed with my plans to recover the Floridas for my king. I will require more cattle for my campaign. Can I count on you to bring back another herd for me?"

"Shouldn't be no problem, now that it's legal to bring 'em in," Ezra said, then he added, "'Course we gotta make us a stop in New Orleans first. Ben, here, is figgerin' on gettin' his self hitched."

The governor's eyes widened in amazement, then he turned to Ben and said, "I did not know you planned to be married. Who is the lucky girl?"

Ben shuffled his feet for a moment, then said, "Happened kind a sudden like. It's Joseph's cousin, Pilar Menchaca."

The governor hesitated before he slowly answered, "An excellent choice, and a beautiful girl. I have known Pilar and her family since she was a child. I find it strange that her father did not mention it when I saw him before coming here." He paused for a moment, then continued, "Now that I think back, Luis told me he was going on a visit to Cuba and Pilar was to go with him. A honeymoon trip as a present, perhaps?"

Ben got to his feet and said, "Doubt it. Her father didn't exactly know about our plans, 'n he was still in Texas, last I heard. Think I better hit the trail for New Orleans."

The governor grabbed Ben's arm and said, "A boat with the wounded leaves within the hour. You will get there much faster if you take it."

"I'll do that, 'n thank you, sir. See you in New Orleans."

Chapter Twenty-Five

BEN SAT WITH HIS BACK against the bulkhead and tried to rest. This was the second night on the river and tomorrow they would arrive in New Orleans. The gentle motion of the vessel as it swayed through the water was soothing, but he was impatient for the journey to end and found it hard to relax.

Uncle Ezra took a seat on the deck and said, "Won't be long now. Reckon what we'll find when we get there?"

"Hard to say. Pilar told me her pa was dead set against us gettin' together, so it'll depend on if she's been able change his mind."

Ezra sent a stream of brown tobacco juice squirting over the side, then asked, "And if she ain't?"

"Try to convince Pilar's father myself, I guess, or just take her and leave. All I know is, I aim to have Pilar."

Ezra grinned and said, "You got it bad all right. Gonna get me some rest. Might need it, come tomorrow."

The Mississippi River disappeared when they were still ten miles upriver from New Orleans, and James Willing, the boat captain, roused Ben out of his blankets with, "Wake up, Mr. Cross. Somethin' ain't right."

Ben sat up in his bed, then feeling no forward movement, he turned and asked, "What's wrong, the boat aground?"

"Might as well be, all the headway we're makin'," the captain grumbled.

Ben rose to his feet, grabbed the steamy mug of coffee pushed at him and said, "Make sense, man. What'n hell you talkin' 'bout?"

"That's just it. Don't know what's goin on. Been on this river, man and boy, near forty years. Current's always strong downstream in this section. Tonight, it's dead against our bow. Slowed us to a crawl. 'Nother thing, the river's rising. Caught sight of the bank in a lightnin' flash, 'n only about half of ten mile oak was clear of water."

The heavy winds and blinding rain of the last two days let up at dawn, but by mid-day the banks of the river could no longer be defied, and they were forced to drop anchor.

Ben stared out over the rail, but all he could see through the fog was murky, churning water.

He walked to the bow where Ezra and Captain Willing were standing and arrived in time to hear his uncle say, "Never seen anythin' like it, Cap. Reckon it's the end o' the world? Not too good on my Scriptures, but I 'member somethin' 'bout a flood."

The captain smiled, then said, "That was in the days of Noah. Supposed to be by fire this time, but the end got here early for a lot of good souls, if what I'm thinking is right."

Ben looked at Jim and asked, "You got this figgered out?"

"Could be, I do. My daddy was a seafaring man most all his life, and told me about giant storms that blow up on the ocean. They're called hurricanes and have strong winds with thirty . . . forty foot waves, and heavy rain. No big deal out on the sea, but on shore, it's a different story.

"My paw was in Jamaica when one hit. Twenty feet of ocean washed over the land, flattened buildings, uprooted trees, and pushed everything ahead of it. Hundreds of people drowned."

"One of then storms is what cost the governor his cattle in the first place," Ezra grumbled.

"You reckon a hurricane caused this?" Ben asked.

The captain trailed his hand over the side, then put his fingers to his mouth and said, "Taste the water."

Ben did so and found it had a salty flavor, then said, "What'd we do now?"

"Nothing to do until the water falls, then we'll go down river and see what's left of New Orleans."

They watched the ocean greedily start to reclaim its own at low tide, sucking the muddy water from the land, and soon the vague outline of the river bank appeared beneath the surface.

Ben wasn't prepared for the devastation revealed by the receding torrent. Huge cypress trees uprooted and twisted in grotesque shapes were scattered around. The bloated bodies of animals dotted the landscape, floated in the water, and snakes were everywhere. Large snakes, small snakes, on the banks, in the water, and all moving in a frenzy, attacking anything that moved. Each other, if no other target was available.

Impatient to get under way, Ben went to the captain and asked, "How long 'fore we move, Jim?"

"Way the water's dropping, a couple hours. Soon as I get me a clear idea where the bank is, we'll weigh anchor."

Their progress was slow when the river fell because Jim was forced to maneuver around snags where fallen trees and debris gathered, and avoid the smashed hulls of overturned vessels.

"She made it," Ezra called out as the boat rounded a bend and he spotted their destination.

Ben grabbed the rail for support when the gentle roll of the boat threw him off balance, then he looked and relief washed over him. New Orleans was still there, at least most of it.

They poled the boat next to a makeshift dock and tied a half hitch around a cleat to hold the vessel in place, then Ben, followed by Ezra and Hacha, jumped ashore and moved hurriedly through the middle of town.

Paco was in front of Joseph's house when the three men walked up the street. The *segundo* had a look of confusion about him, but greeted them warmly, then asked, "How is it you are here? The governor's campaign is expected to last many months. Do things go badly for our troops?"

Ezra rolled the tobacco around in his mouth and sent a stream of brown liquid squirting to the cobblestones, then grinned and said, "Not hardly. War's over, leastway's where we come from. We whipped the Redcoats, 'n the whole damn Mississippi's in Spanish hands. The army's on it's way here t' get ready 'n attack the British in Florida."

A big smile spread over Paco's face and he said, "*Magnifico*, but how can this be so?"

"Later, my friend," Ben said, "Where are the others? "Hacha's anxious t' see Paloma. I'll explain 'bout the fightin' when we're all together."

Paco looked at him with somber eyes, then turned to Hacha and said, "She is here. Come inside, all of you. There is much I have to tell."

Ben felt his belly muscles tighten as he entered the house, then he grabbed Paco's arm and asked, "What's wrong? Where's Pilar? Where's Joseph?"

"Sit down, *hermano*. Pilar is not here. She has gone to Cuba. Her father insisted she go with him to Havana to pay her respects to her grandfather. Pilar left this for you."

Ben was stunned. He accepted the envelope from Paco, then unfolded the letter and stared at the writing on the page.

Mi Amor,
   I pray you never read these words. If you do, it will mean you have completed your mission before my return. I would prefer to explain in person why I felt compelled to go to Havana, but left this letter for you in case I am delayed.
   My grandfather who lives in Cuba is very ill.

*and not expected to survive. His dying wish is to
see me and, as his only granddaughter, I could not
refuse to go.*

*I have spoken to my father about us, and even
though his choice for me is someone Spanish, I
have told him I will have no one but you. I am
happy to report that* mi padre *is now convinced of
my feelings, and has withdrawn his objection to
our marriage.*

*I beg your understanding of why I am not here,
and will miss you terribly.*

Until we are together again, I remain always
> *yours,*
> *all my love,*
> *Pilar*

He carefully closed the page, then his uncle touched Ben
on the arm and gently asked, "What'd she have t' say, boy?"

Ben explained what Pilar had written and Ezra said,
"Ain't so bad. She'll be back 'fore you know it."

He put the letter in his pocket then turned to Paco and
said, "Need to see Joseph. Governor wants us to get him
some more longhorns."

"My *patrón* is no longer in New Orleans. He left for the
rancho with a wagon train of goods from the clipper ship."

Ben jerked his head up and asked, "Joseph's gone? What
in hell's he haulin' that he had t' get back so quick, 'n why
ain't you with 'em?"

"Joseph ordered me to wait here for you to see if additional cattle would be required. I did not wish to remain.
My place is with my *patrón*, and I worry for his safety."

Ezra looked for a place to spit, but found none, then
swallowed the tobacco juice in his mouth and asked, "How
come? Didn't he take enough men?"

"Yes *señor*, many men, but that kind of danger is not
what I worry about."

Ben's face screwed up in a frown, but he didn't say anything, and Paco continued, "As you know, Texas and Louisiana are both Spanish provinces, but trade is not permitted between them, so we are forced to get many things we need at the *rancho* from Mexico City. That takes many months, and supplies are sometimes short. New Orleans is much closer, and now that cattle can be transported, my *patrón* believes other trade will be opened soon, but for now, he illegally takes a train of much needed goods to the people of *Rancho de San Francisco*."

Ben asked, "What'll happen if he's caught?"

Paco shrugged his shoulders and said, "The governor of Texas and the Menchaca family are political enemies. If Joseph were not who he is, a small fine and confiscation of the goods would be the punishment, but if he is discovered, the authorities will use the incident to embarrass the family, maybe even to arrest the *patrón*."

Ben thought for a moment, then said, "Nothin' to do about it now. Maybe he'll get through. We'll find out when we get back t' Texas. Stock up on supplies, 'n have the men ready. This is Tuesday. We're gonna pull out of here by the weekend."

THE SOUND OF loud knocking roused Ben from his slumber in the pre-dawn hours of Friday morning. He climbed out of bed and opened the door to find a Spanish soldier in the hall.

The man handed Ben a note, then turned on his heel to leave as Ezra rolled out of his blankets and asked, "What's all the noise 'bout?"

Ben read the message, then handed it to his uncle and said, "Governor's back, 'n wants to see us. Says to come now."

Ezra scratched his chin and said, "Must be important to wake us this early. 'Spect we better get on over there."

Ben glanced up to see the sun start to rise over the horizon as they arrived at the palace. Ezra got rid of his excess tobacco juice before they went inside, then they entered to find Oliver Pollock and several other men in the office with the governor.

Ben looked around, then asked, "What'd you need to see me about, Governor?"

"Sit down, my boy. I'm afraid I have some bad news," then the governor motioned to a distinguished looking gentleman on his right and said, "This is Luis Menchaca, Pilar's father."

Ben's mouth dropped open and he was stunned into silence.

Ezra blurted out, "Pilar's father? Thought he was on a boat with Pilar headin' for Cuba."

Ben grabbed Menchaca's arm and asked, "What's happened? Where's Pilar?"

The old man looked at Ben with sadness in his eyes and said, "She's gone. My daughter is gone forever."

"Gone! What in hell you talkin' 'bout?" Ben demanded.

The governor stepped between the two men and said, "Calm down, Ben. It was an accident. This is Miguel Guerra, ship *capitán* of the 'Crescent.' He will explain."

The captain turned to Ben said, "My vessel, she runs into a storm, *señor*, when we are only one day out of port. The same one that hits here, I think. The ship is blown far to the west and heavily damaged by the raging seas. Many lifeboats washed overboard and only two remained when the 'Crescent' started to take on water and began to sink. I ordered the women and children into the small boats, along with a few able-bodied seamen, then launched them off the Texas coast. I thought it their only chance to survive."

Ezra interrupted, "If the boat was a sinkin', like ya say, 'n you stayed with it, how come you fellers're here?"

The captain said, "The 'Crescent' was still afloat after the storm passed and the crew made temporary repairs. We sailed along the Texas coast as we limped back to port, but saw no sign of survivors. No fires or even remains of the lifeboats."

Ben asked, with disgust in his voice, "You didn't send a party ashore to search, I guess?"

The captain held out his hands and said, "Would that I could, *señor*, but we had no lifeboats, and a shortage of men. The 'Crescent', itself, barely made it back to New Orleans."

Ben's brain was in a whirl and numb at the same time. Pilar dead? His mind just couldn't accept that as fact, but there was only one way to know for sure.

He turned to the governor and asked, "You got another ship? One that'll drop me off on the Texas coast?"

The governor put his hand on Ben's shoulder and said, "Of a certainty I do, and I know how you must feel, but what you attempt is folly. We don't know if the boats made it to shore."

We don't know they didn't, neither," Ezra piped in. "I'm with ya, boy, 'n Hacha'll want a go too. I'll go fetch him."

Ben turned to the governor and said, "Like to leave soon as I can. Send Paco back for the cattle. He'll get 'em through for you. I'll take Pilar back to Texas when I find her. Don't 'spect you to understand, but I know in my heart that Pilar's alive. She's out there somewhere 'n I mean to find her."

Luis Menchaca stared sadly at Ben for a moment, then slowly said, "Go with God."